CW00339554

THE DOUBLECROSS GUN

Matt Vickers, deputy United States marshal, was a quiet man, but he attracted trouble as a dog attracts fleas. At thirty, he had spent a third of his life as a lawman. Now he was on the most dangerous mission of all, but one that was more than a mere job—because it involved a friend.

Peter B. Germano was born the oldest of six children in New Bedford, Massachusetts. During the Great Depression, he had to go to work before completing high school. It left him with a powerful drive to continue his formal education later in life, finally earning a Master's degree from Loyola University in Los Angeles in 1970. He sold his first Western story to A.A. Wyn's Ace Publishing magazine group when he was twenty years old. In the same issue of *Sure-Fire Western* (1/39) Germano had two stories, one by Peter Germano and the other by Barry Cord. He came to prefer the Barry Cord name for his Western fiction. When the Second World War came, he joined the U.S. Marine Corps. Following the war he would be called back to active duty, again as a combat correspondent, during the Korean conflict. In 1948 Germano began publishing a series of Western novels, either as Barry Cord or **Jim Kane**, stories notable for their complex plots while the scenes themselves are simply set, with a minimum of description and quick character sketches employed to establish a wide assortment of very different personalities. The pacing, which often seems swift due to the adept use of a parallel plot structure (narrating a story from several different viewpoints), is combined in these novels with atmospheric descriptions of weather and terrain. *Dry Range* (1955), *The Sagebrush Kid* (1954), *The Iron Trail Killers* (1960), and *Trouble in Peaceful Valley* (1968) are among his best Westerns. "The great southwest . . ." Germano wrote in 1982, "this is the country, and these are the people that gripped my imagination . . . and this is what I have been writing about for forty years. And until I die I shall remain the little New England boy who fell in love with the 'West,' and as a man had the opportunity to see it and live in it."

THE DOUBLECROSS GUN

James Kane

GUNSMOKE

First published in the UK by Robert Hale Ltd.

This hardback edition 2003
by BBC Audiobooks Ltd
by arrangement with
Golden West Literary Agency

ISBN 0 7540 8240 7

British Library Cataloguing in Publication Data available.

Printed and bound in Great Britain by
Antony Rowe Ltd., Chippenham, Wiltshire

– 1 –

AGAINST THE FALL of night the barn thrust its stone and log shoulder, dropping its squat black shadow into the trampled dust where three men sat on tired horses.

Over them loomed the heavy oak beam which had served as a hoist for bales of hay stored in the loft. Less than a week ago it had served as a gallows for Sheriff Tom Billens, as tough a lawman as any who had ever worn a Texas badge.

The barn was all that remained of Bev Walker's horse spread. The barn had been burned down to its foundations, and rain poked its moist fingers through the embers.

Bev Walker had been the sheriff's friend.

Matt Vickers, deputy U.S. marshal, broodingly eyed the charred timbers. He was a tall, wide-shouldered man with a rider's build, lean-flanked, wiry, and a lawman's objective, almost fatalistic slant on life. He was thirty, and for a third of his lifetime he had worn a federal officer's star. He was a quiet man who was seldom at peace; his job kept him moving toward trouble, and he was headed for it now. But this time it was colored by sentiment, for Sheriff Billens had been an old friend.

He took a last drag at his limp cigaret and snapped the butt into the charred ruins. His voice was brittle.

"We'll separate here. You go in first, Kip. Ride in from the east. Take your time; drift into the Pecos Bar. I'll see you there."

Kip Billens, tall and lanky and sleepy-eyed, nodded. He had a careless slouch in the saddle. He had a small Mexican cheroot between his lips which he never lighted. He liked the taste of the strong tobacco, not the smoke. He was in his late twenties—a hard, sandy-bearded, cold-eyed man with a single gun thonged down on his left hip.

Kip laid his glance on the rails which ran past empty corrals of the horse spread. The sun was on his left, gone down behind the broken horizon. Against the low hills the town of Fulton was a vague pattern pricked by lamplight.

Kip raised his hand in a brief parting gesture, touched his heels to his leggy steeldust mare and jogged away from them.

The federal officer watched Kip hit the rail bed and head his cayuse toward town.

"We'll give him twenty minutes," Matt said. "Then you take the south trail in, Doc. We'll meet at the same place."

Doc Emory nodded. He was a slightly built man with thin brown hair, thin cheeks, quick brown eyes. He was in his late forties, but looked older. He wore no gun belt, but there were few men in Texas who could beat him to the draw with the .38 Smith & Wesson in his shoulder holster.

Doc was an ex-Texas Ranger. He had drifted into the Lone Star State from Kansas—a close-mouthed, silent man. He said he was a dentist; he did carry a few professional tools in a black bag strapped to his saddle.

Matt had never known him to practice dentistry. Doc was better at cards—a cool hand at poker, a deadly man with a gun. On the surface he was a quiet-spoken, mild-mannered man, but he was subject to violent rages which erupted often with little warning. He had worn a Ranger's badge for less than a year when he killed a man over a woman in a Laredo hostelry and sent in his resignation to Ranger headquarters.

Now he sat moody and silent, staring after Kip. He said without looking at Matt: "You know what you're going up against, Matt?"

Vickers nodded. "The worst guns in Texas!" His voice was curt.

"Luke McQuade!" Doc's voice held a thin sarcasm. "Killed four men in the Lincoln County war, three up at that Montana sheepmen fracas. The Earps gave him elbow room at Dodge City. Bat Masterson left town the day Luke rode into Abilene."

Matt Vickers made no comment. He was looking at the town nestled in the shadows of the low hills. He wasn't thinking of Luke McQuade. He was remembering Marty Rawlings, U.S. marshal, who had ridden into Fulton to investigate Sheriff Billens' death and had been found in an alley two days later with bullets in his back.

Doc stirred, sensing his companion's somber mood. His lips twisted bitterly. "The men Luke brought with him are almost as bad. They own the town; they run it! Billens tried to buck them and wound up swinging at the end of his own rope. Oh, I know there were no witnesses, Matt, just like no one saw who killed Rawlings. But there's no law in Fulton now except Luke McQuade's law!"

His words seemed to make no impression on the tall federal officer. The little man shifted in the saddle and sighed.

"It ain't only the town, is it, Matt? It's the railroad big Chris Marlowe is building through here, the Desert Line. A lot of people have sunk money in Marlowe's wildcat venture. He has to get track across the Creosote Strip to Black Wells, or he and the railroad will go broke."

Doc's glance swung out to the dark hills. "He's not going to make it, Matt. Big Chris Marlowe won't finish laying track across the Strip, because McQuade won't let him."

Matt turned to the small man then, a cold light gleaming fitfully in his strange, amber-colored eyes. "If you feel that way, Doc, why did you come along?"

Doc eyed Matt, his regard cold and remote. He was like a turtle who, sensing danger, suddenly pulls his head back within his shell.

"I've got nothing to lose," he said finally. "Tom Billens was a friend of mine, too." He let it go at that, but there was more, unsaid, running through his mind.

He had reached the end of the trail in more ways than one. He had had two attacks since that day he had turned in his Ranger badge. The last time the doctor had warned him, "Next time will be your last. Take it easy, and your heart might last another couple of years."

But it wasn't this that was bothering Doc Emory, nor Luke McQuade's guns.

He was thinking of the man who had just left them. He had lied to Matt Vickers about this man, and it did not set easily on him.

"Why are you here, Matt?" he countered.

The federal officer's gaze was on the barely visible rails stretching toward Fulton. Under the prod of the little man's question, those rails seemed to run into infinity. They became the iron road to a thousand frontier towns, became the symbols of the iron bonds of duty. He had no reason to be there, and yet he had more reason than Kip Billens, whose brother, Sheriff Billens, had been killed there—more reason than Doc Emory had. For Matt Vickers was there because it was his job; because pinned to the inside of his wallet he carried a federal officer's badge, and he was the kind of man who took his job seriously.

So his answer was that simple: "It's my job, Doc."

"A hundred a month!" Doc Emory's laughter was rude. "I know a half-dozen men who'd be glad to pay you five times that much and think they were getting a bargain."

Matt shrugged. Money was all right for the kind of man who wanted only what money could buy. What he wanted could not be bought with money. The wry thought came to him often that what he wanted could only be bought with lead.

He let silence fall between him and the little man. Matt had not known Doc Emory too well.

Doc sensed Matt's mood; he said softly, "See you in the Pecos Bar, Matt."

Vickers watched the little man turn his horse, ride into the long shadows and fade away toward the south.

Sitting saddle, alone now, Matt reflected bleakly that the worst congregation of killers in Texas seemed to have come to Fulton. They had taken over the railroad town, and they seemed out to smash Marlowe's Desert Line.

Moreover, they held an unbeatable hand.

Somewhere in Fulton or in the badlands of the Creosote Strip, they were holding Big Chris Marlowe's wife and daughter as hostages.

Marlowe was an influential man in Texas—a big man who had started out as a bull wagon driver and freighter and switched early to the greater promise of the iron rails. The Desert Line, however, was his first independent venture.

It looked as if it would be his last. Marlowe might have been able to influence the governor to send the militia to Fulton, but there was no actual evidence against Luke McQuade and his bunch. And the unsigned, scrawled note Marlowe had received after his wife's and daughter's disappearance, warning him that his family would die if he made a move in that direction, had stopped the big railroad man.

It was that note he had brought into the district marshal's office when he had asked for federal help.

As Doc Emory had pointed out, there was no evidence that Luke McQuade was behind the kidnaping, or connected with the hanging of Sheriff Billens or the killing of Marty Rawlings. If there had been any witnesses, they were not talking.

But what was it Luke McQuade wanted in Fulton? Was it his idea to break the Desert Line? What would a gunslinger like McQuade stand to gain from it?

These questions bothered Marshal Matt Vickers.

He thought of the hard-faced Kip Billens and of Doc Emory. And the cold edge of caution chilled him. Matt tried to rationalize the feeling away. He worked alone too often; he was needlessly suspicious.

It had not been his original intention to ride into Fulton with Kip Billens or Emory. He had run into Doc in Paseo, and Emory had sensed where Matt was headed. The ex-Ranger had been quick to lay his proposition before Matt.

"Meet Kip Billens," he had said. "Tom Billens was his brother." The explanation was simple. Doc and Kip were riding to Fulton. Doc was going because he liked the younger Billens; Kip was riding to avenge his brother.

It was that simple—and that complicated.

"You run the show, Matt," they had agreed. "But even you can use a couple of extra guns against McQuade and his bunch. What do you say?"

Vickers had hesitated. Then Kip's level voice had come hard across the table:

"Whatever you say, Marshal. I'm headed for Fulton regardless. We can work together, or I'll work alone!"

So Matt had taken on company.

He sat now, the big blue roan moving restlessly under him. He felt inside his pocket, brought out a coin, and examined it in the poor light.

It was an old Spanish *reale,* sometimes called "pieces of eight" because they ran eight to the peso. This one had a notch in the rim, cut with a triangular file.

It had come to district headquarters on the day he was leaving. The note with it had been addressed to the district marshal; it was written in a plainly feminine hand.

Give this to the next man you send down to Fulton. Have him show it to the bartender in the Pecos Bar. It will tell him where he can find Mrs. Marlowe and her daughter.

The unsigned note had come by way of Texas Ranger headquarters, with a suggestion that a federal officer from out of the state might be less conspicuous in Fulton than another Texas

Ranger. They would stand by with immediate help, when and if Vickers located the Marlowe women.

Vickers eyed the old Spanish coin with bleak thoughtfulness. Maybe this was the key that would break Luke McQuade.

There was only one way to find out. Matt touched heels lightly to the roan's flanks and headed for Fulton.

THE MAN CALLED Kip Billens followed the rails toward Fulton and cut away from them before he reached town. He seemed to know where he was going. He rode through the darkness, and when he came to the first thin scattering of buildings he swung wide and followed an unseen trail toward a shack sitting on a slight slope overlooking the town. He rode up and reined in a dozen feet from the closed door. He made no move to dismount. There was no light in the shack, but this did not bother him.

He waited without impatience, the cheroot dangling from his lips. After a while the door opened, but the interior blackness soaked up all the outlines of the man in the doorway; he was a vague and shapeless hulk with a commanding, harsh voice.

"Yes?"

"He's here," Kip said.

The man in the doorway did not move, but an air of satisfaction emanated from him and touched the man on horseback.

Kip's hand drifted down to his gun butt, "When?"

"I'll let you know," the man snapped. Then, after a moment, he added softly: "I knew he'd come, Lou."

"Kip Billens," the sandy-haired man said **softly.**

"Oh, yes—Kip." The unseen man's voice was amused. "A loaded gun at his side, and Matt Vickers doesn't suspect a thing." His laughter had a grim edge. "This is one job that United States marshal won't get to finish!"

The man called Kip made no comment. He had long ago trained himself to keep his thoughts to himself, to eye the present coldly and to suspect the future.

"How did you convince Doc?"

"Emory?" The gunman shrugged. "He's—he owes me something." His voice was flat and sour in the night.

The man in the doorway hesitated. "I'll get word to you later. Find out who Vickers contacts."

He closed the door. The gunman sat saddle for a moment, the darkness hiding the lines in his face. When he turned the steeldust, it was with an unaccustomed and abrupt savagery, as if something distasteful had come up to bother him.

Doc Emory came into the town of Fulton from the south. He rode loosely in the saddle, an old man not caring what other people might think. He had failed the law once before, and now he was bitter at the thought that he might fail it again.

He knew who the man he had called Kip Billens really was. Could he trust him? Inside him was an old deep hurt; he thought of the Biblical line, *"Blood is thicker than water."*

Was it thicker than duty, more binding than self-respect?

He cursed himself for his weakness, and the lie he had foisted on Matt Vickers.

THE DIAMOND-STACKED engine stood on the siding by the small depot, its boilers hissing in the night. A switchman waved his lantern. The engine let out steam and backed into the darkness, meeting the first of the three box cars waiting in the night. The clash of iron couplings rang out in the gloom, muting the girl's sharp cry.

Vickers was cutting across the tracks in front of the depot when he heard the girl scream, and instinctively he swung the blue roan toward the sound.

The station was a long oblong set down along the rails. It stood apart from the town; it was like a small settlement in itself, clinging to the gleaming rails. Loading corrals and tool sheds cast their dark shadows behind it.

The vast hissing of the engine, now moving

slowly toward him, drowned out any further sound. For a moment the U.S. marshal was tempted to let it ride that way. He had no wish to get involved in trouble even before he entered the rail town.

But the echoes of the cry pulled him toward the depot. His horse stepped a little nervously as the engine rolled past them. Steam billowed up and enveloped them, then faded away.

A yellow-wheeled buggy was pulled up in the shadows of the depot; a saddled horse stood patiently in front of it.

On the small platform running along the front of the depot to the warehouse shed, a dark figure moved hurriedly. He passed through the lamp glow from the waiting room windows, and Matt saw a spare-bodied, middle-aged man in shirt sleeves and dark vest. A gold watch chain looped across his vest glinted briefly in the light.

The man turned abruptly into the station. The heavy wheels of the freight made a noise in the night, but the panting of the engine did not drown out the girl's cry that came from inside the station.

Vickers pulled his mettlesome stallion in toward the depot and dropped from the saddle, ground-reining the animal. He put his palms on the waist-high platform and went up like a cat. He was headed for the waiting room door when the engine, backing up again, billowed vapor over the platform.

The small waiting room was empty, save for the sprawled figure by the railing fencing off the office area. Beyond this railing were four people.

A white-haired man wearing a green eyeshade sat behind a small desk, his lips tight with helpless anger. Near him, his buttocks resting on the low railing, lounged a short, stocky figure. He had his hand on his gun butt, but he was watching the man and the girl up by the back wall, and he did not immediately see Vickers enter.

The girl was backed into a corner of the small office. She was a slim girl in a skirt and shirtwaist and obviously worked there. The man facing her had a rangy build and was encased in tight-fitting town clothes; he had his back to the door and was relying on the stocky man to cut off any interference.

The girl's hand was upraised, her fingers curled tightly around a lead paperweight. Her voice was high, desperate.

"One step closer, Ret, and I'll—"

The man's hand stabbed out and closed around her slim wrist. He twisted it, and as he pulled her to him she uttered a sharp cry and dropped the weight. She averted her face from his seeking mouth and beat against his chest with her free hand.

The stocky man on the railing now caught a glimpse of the U.S. marshal out of the corner of his eye. His voice sent a warning back as he slid around on the railing to face Vickers.

"Ret, we got company!"

He was lifting his Colt out of the holster in a quick movement when Vickers' palm heeled sharply against his square jaw. The weight of the tall lawman's shoulder was behind it. Shorty hit the railing and flipped over it, his boots coming up high over his head. He landed on the back of his neck on the office side of the floor, and his Colt went sliding under a bench desk. For the next few moments he lost all interest in what went on inside the station.

The man called Ret whirled, his hand dipping inside his town coat. It froze there, his eyes looking down into the muzzle of Matt's leveled gun.

The girl stumbled away from him, her quick cry causing Vickers' eyes to narrow. He made a motion with his Colt.

"All right, Romeo. Looks like Juliet doesn't want to play. Beat it!"

A bright anger strained against the caution in the rangy town man's gaze. He looked awkward in the town suit. He had a stolid, weathered face, and he might have been in his mid-twenties, but he looked older. He was bareheaded, and his yellow hair was parted in the middle and slicked down; under his curved beak of a nose, a thick brown mustache was neatly trimmed.

He balanced on his toes, his thick-muscled hands clenching slowly. "This is a private affair, mister," he snarled. "Keep out of it!"

Matt kept his eyes on the man, but his voice was directed to the girl. "Just to make sure I'm not butting in where I don't belong, was this slicked-up tinhorn bothering you, miss?"

The girl was at the desk by the white-haired man wearing the green eyeshade. She turned to Matt, nodded, then found her voice. "Yes!"

Matt's eyes carried a bleak warning. "All right, mister. You heard the lady. Pick up your fat friend and get out of here!"

Ret Blue ignored Vickers. He turned to face the girl, anger choking his voice. "I came peaceful tonight, Betty. I want you to remember this. Hired a buggy. Even brung you a present."

The girl stepped away from the desk to the small ledger bench. There was a small square box on it, tied with a pink ribbon. She picked it up and threw it at the man.

"Take your present, Ret. I've never asked for any. Nor have I ever given you reason to believe I would welcome any, or you!"

Ret turned to the marshal. At his feet Shorty was beginning to show signs of life. Ret bent, helped the man up and shoved him toward the railing gate.

Shorty stumbled through, looked at Matt and dropped his hand to his empty holster. The rangy man came up quickly and shouldered him away. "Later, Shorty," he promised harshly. "We'll settle with him later."

He stopped in the doorway. The impression persisted in Vickers that this man was out of place in his tight-fitting town clothes. His flat dull face burned with a violent anger.

"We've got a place in town for jaspers like you, mister—gents who don't mind their own business! It's six foot long and three foot deep!"

Vickers drifted toward the door, the hammer

of his Colt clicking audibly under his thumb. "Stick around," he said softly, "and I'll help you fill it."

MATT VICKERS waited in the shadows of the station platform until Ret climbed into the buggy. Shorty hauled himself stiffly into the saddle of the waiting horse; he rubbed the back of his neck and glanced at the U.S. marshal, studying him with a narrowed gaze. Vickers wasn't wearing his badge openly, and there was nothing to indicate that he was other than a stranger who had stuck his nose into business that didn't concern him. Shorty's gaze clung to Vickers for a long moment; then both men swung away from the platform and headed for town.

The girl was kneeling by the man on the floor when Matt returned. She was brushing thin hair back from the gash above the man's right eye. It was an ugly bruise, bleeding slightly, matting the hair around it.

She turned to face Matt. "This is my father," she said. "Shorty hit him with his gun when he came in."

"Let me take a look at him," Matt suggested. He crouched beside her and probed the scalp cut with long gentle fingers. The older man groaned. His eyes opened, but for the first few seconds they were plainly out of focus.

Matt turned to the oldster with the green eye-shade. "Is there a doctor in town?" At the man's nod he said, "Get him."

The billing clerk hurried out.

The girl was frightened. "Is Dad badly hurt?"

Matt frowned. "I think he'll have a bad headache for a day or two. But I'm not a doctor, and he might have a concussion, Miss—"

"Betty Grover," she answered. "My father is Paul Grover, station agent."

Grover was trying to get up. Matt steadied him, holding the older man when he sagged against the railing. The station agent put his hand up to his eyes, as if the lamplight hurt them.

"Where are they, Betty? Where's Ret?" He turned to look at Vickers. "Who is this man?" His words were little more than a pained mumble between his fingers.

"Ret's gone," Betty answered. "This is—" She looked askance at the marshal.

"Matt," Vickers said. "The rest of it doesn't matter, does it?"

Betty smiled. Her eyes made an appraisal of

the lawman, and she liked what she saw. She put
that liking into her blue eyes, her voice.

"He made Ret and Shorty leave," she told her
father. "He's sent Fred for Doctor Blake."

Paul Grover dropped his hands to the railing for support and surveyed Vickers. "Thanks,
Matt." His lips stiffened. "Head's pounding like
a triphammer," he muttered.

Vickers helped him to a bench. In the lamplight Paul Grover looked somewhat shriveled,
his sallow face muddy.

"Stranger in Fulton, aren't you?"

Vickers nodded.

"Thanks for interfering," the old man said.
"You were more effective than I was." Grover
paused to take in a breath. "I heard Betty cry
out and blundered in. Shorty nearly split my
skull." His tone was low, bitter. "Don't know
what your business in Fulton may be, Matt, but
take my advice—leave. Right now."

"Why?" Matt's voice was even. "Because of
Ret and Shorty?"

Grover nodded. "Ret Blue is Luke McQuade's
half-brother. McQuade runs Fulton. Or didn't
you know?"

"I heard."

Something in the lawman's voice made Grover raise his head. He studied Vickers, seeing a big man, hard-muscled, quiet—a gunman without bravado, deadly, sure of himself. He looked much like the killers who had taken over Fulton. And yet there was something in Matt Vickers' face, in the regard of his blue-gray eyes, that was different; something he could not pin down. Yet it was a reassuring quality, and it gave Grover a buoyancy he could not understand.

"What did Ret come in here for?" Matt asked.

Betty Grover flushed. "He came to take me riding. He's Luke McQuade's half-brother, and he thinks that gives him the right to—"

"He's been pestering Betty for some time now," Paul said. "I told him to leave her alone. But—" his jaws clamped hard—"there's only one way to make Ret understand. I'm buying me a Winchester tomorrow."

Matt remembered Ret's move toward his shoulder gun, the look in his eyes. Paul Grover would be dead the moment he reached for that rifle, unless Grover meant to shoot Ret in the back. And the station agent didn't strike Matt as that kind of a man.

He thought of this, and then he remembered

why he had come to Fulton. Paul Grover's problems would have to take care of themselves. . . .

He had first to locate a woman and a girl and get them safely away from Luke McQuade. He had to find out why McQuade was holding up construction of a rail line that could mean nothing to him.

And he had to find out if the note which had accompanied the notched coin in his pocket meant what it said. Or could it be a trap?

Fred came in just then with the doctor, a tall, rumpled, slender man, not yet thirty. He looked searchingly at Matt before bending over Grover and making an examination.

"You've got a hard head, Paul," he told the station agent. "You'll have a headache for two or three days." He turned and smiled reassuringly at Betty. The doctor had a boyish, pleasant face when he smiled.

"Maybe this will convince you, Paul," he continued, working swiftly with scissors, cutting away blood-matted hair from around the gash. "Get out of Fulton. The Desert Line's bankrupt. Take Betty with you."

"Not as long as I'm the station agent," Paul said stubbornly. "Not until Mr. Marlowe tells me he's through. There's close to five hundred men at Track Town who are still depending on Chris Marlowe to come through. I'm not going to run out on them."

Matt shrugged slightly and said: "Guess I'll be going." He headed for the door, remembering his appointment at the Pecos Bar.

Betty turned to him. "Matt, I really haven't had time to thank you."

Matt smiled. "Some other time. Tomorrow, perhaps. If my business in Fulton doesn't work out, I might ask your father for a job on the railroad."

He saw Doctor Blake scowl; it might have been because of the girl. He had a young man's possessiveness about Betty Grover.

Paul Grover nodded. "I could use you, Matt." He made a weary gesture with his hands. "But I'm afraid you've already put yourself to a lot of trouble."

"Used to it," Matt murmured. He nodded briefly and stepped outside.

In the night the engine, its freight made up, was beginning to roll east. Its whistle came back to Matt in a long, hauntingly lonely wail.

– III –

TO BETTY GROVER, the dingy railroad station office seemed oddly unsafe after the tall man left it. Fred was standing by, small and helpless, his green eyeshade casting a sickly glow across his lined features.

She looked at her father and Roger Blake and read in their eyes the same feelings; the night seemed lonely and frightening, and the fading wail of the train touched off a slight shiver in her.

Doctor Blake saw it and straightened, his jaw jutting with faint bitterness. He said: "Paul, for the last time, get out of Fulton. Or send Betty away, at least."

Grover sighed. "I'm not leaving, Roger. I've got my job here. I can't quit on Marlowe now." He turned to his daughter, but she forestalled his request.

"No," she said stubbornly. "I'm staying here with you."

She turned to Roger Blake, eying the young railroad doctor in a new appraisal. He was as tall as the man who called himself Matt, and there was a stubborn slant to the line of his jaw that she liked. He was capable, too. But his capabilities ran along other lines from those needed in Fulton now; she saw his realization of his deficiencies in his troubled eyes, and she did not judge him harshly for it. But it was the stranger who had just left who made her feel protected, satisfied her feminine need of masculine strength, roused her.

Blake seemed to sense her thoughts. His hands clenched helplessly; he turned to Paul Grover. "I'm not a fighting man, Paul." He seemed ashamed. "I'm a doctor. I came to Fulton to work for the railroad." He didn't add that he had remained because of Betty, but it was apparent in his voice.

He picked up his medical bag, his lips tightening. "I have a pistol in my office. From now on I'm going to take it with me. If Ret or any other of those toughs who have taken over this town bother you again, Betty—"

She quickly put a hand on his arm. "No, Roger. They'd kill you!"

His face reddened. "You know the way I feel about you," he said quietly, "and you saw what happened tonight. Ret will be back. He's not the kind of man who will stay away from what he wants." The young doctor's voice was thick with anger and frustration. "If you won't leave town, then there's no other choice for me." He added bitterly, "The next time Ret comes around, this man who calls himself Matt may not be around."

"Roger—" Betty's eyes were soft, smiling a little—"I'm grateful. And I do know how you feel about me. But I can't leave Dad. And I don't think Ret will be bothering me again."

Her voice was firm, but she really did not believe it.

Grover came to his feet. "I've got a feeling Ret's troubles are just beginning," he interrupted. "Roger, take Betty home for me. Stay for supper."

Doctor Blake nodded. "Glad to, Paul." He added, "I'm driving out to Track Town tomorrow. Want me to see Mike Flannagan for you?"

Grover nodded absently. "Tell Mike to keep the boys working. I'm waiting for word from

Marlowe now; tell them I expect a payroll in by the weekend. Tell Mike anything, but make that big mick promise to keep the crew working on that *arroyo blanco* fill."

Blake's smile was a little stiff. He took Betty's arm, and she walked with him a little reluctantly. At the door she turned. "Sarah will have supper ready, Dad. Don't keep us waiting."

She made it a question, and Paul nodded impatiently, his eyes squinting as the movement brought a sharp pounding between them. He watched Roger and his daughter leave; then, after a moment, he walked to the door and looked out.

The night wind had a dampness in it; it smelled of rain. He stood in the doorway and listened to the occasional shots which drifted to him from town. Remembering the two men who had invaded his office and forced themselves on Betty, he suddenly felt impotent and afraid.

He had not realized what it meant to be afraid, to be helpless, until Sheriff Tom Billens had been killed and his deputy, gun-whipped and broken physically, had left town.

Suddenly there was no longer order in Fulton, only fear and a nagging helplessness.

He had wired Marlowe about the situation

right after the first work train had been dynamited off the rails on its way to the end of the track. A deputy U.S. marshal named Rawlings had come to see him and had asked questions. Two days later his body had been found in an alley.

Grover's thoughts followed the twin rails into the darkness. The men at Track Town were working half-heartedly. Mike Flannagan was a good construction foreman. But how long could he keep his crew working on the promise of wages already long delayed?

Dissatisfied and tired, Paul Grover went back inside his office. Fred was working on a small pile of bills of lading, scratching conscientiously with his quill pen. Grover walked to the iron safe in a corner of the office and crouched before it. Opening the heavy door, he took out the wire he had received from Chris Marlowe three days before. Marlowe had sent it himself, in code, and though Fred had taken down the message only Paul knew what it said.

He read it again for confirmation.

Payroll arriving on special train due in Fulton at eight o'clock Wednesday evening. Absolute secrecy essential. Trusting you to get it through to men at Track Town. Marlowe.

Grover sighed heavily and put the wire back in the safe and locked it. Turning, he noticed Fred watching him. He made a wry face.

"No hurry on those bills, Fred," he said. "Let's lock up and go home."

He walked to the door and paused on the outside platform, his thoughts suddenly occupied by the image of the tall, wide-shouldered man who had so opportunely ridden by earlier that night.

"Just Matt," the man had said. He could be anyone; quite probably he was a killer with a reputation. A lot of them had been drifting into Fulton lately.

Yet for no good reason, Paul didn't believe this. Instead, remembering the man's quiet assurance, his spirits lifted; he walked with a lighter step toward the end of the platform.

DEPOT AVENUE led Matt Vickers into Fulton. A few months before the dusty road had petered out at the *barranca*, which had placed a natural limit to the town's expansion in that direction.

Then the iron rails had come to Fulton, and overnight the town had hurdled the gully and pushed its ramshackle and jerry-built structures across and into the gopher-holed prairie beyond.

Now a heavy plank bridge extended Depot Avenue across the deep-shadowed moat into the blatancy of Fulton's new section.

The Pecos Bar stood on the corner facing the bridge and the old town, like a prematurely old man bracing himself for the effort of crossing. Its unpainted wooden bulk, with a low wing jutting incongruously from its side, loomed up against the bright splatter of stars. The light of a late-rising moon, hidden behind it, fashioned a sort of reddish halo over the ugly structure. Or perhaps, Matt reflected bleakly, it was a faint reflection of hell.

It was a wide-open town now that Sheriff Billens was dead. The night was split at sporadic intervals by gunshots, more often by the drunken shouts of brawling men. Most of the disturbances came from across the bridge; in contrast, the dark huddle of buildings at Matt's back seemed desolate and depressingly quiet.

The ragged outline of the new section stirred a faint resentment in the U.S. marshal. He was as alert as a lobo on a down-wind trail, and a warning chill touched him, borne on the wings of the night.

He did not fool himself. No man was invulnerable to a bullet in the back, or a shotgun blast from the covering darkness of an alley.

But until it became known who he was, he would be given a certain freedom of movement. He would be eyed and weighed. And in that small measure of time he would have to find out who was holding Marlowe's wife and daughter captive, learn who was behind the holdup of the Desert Line.

The plank boomed hollowly under the big stallion's hoofs as they crossed the bridge. A piano banged out a dance tune in the Pecos Bar, the music barely audible above the hooting voices inside. Over the slatted doors a flickering lamp cast its uncertain light across the black-lettered sign.

Vickers swung his horse in toward the crowded tie-rack, nosing the stallion alongside Doc's gray. Kip's steeldust was at the rail, slack-hipped and drowsy.

Dismounting, the marshal walked to the entrance. He palmed the batwings and walked into a big smoke-filled room, noisy with talk. Most of the noise was concentrated toward the rear of the room, where a half-dozen girls in spangled tights were kicking to the tune of a piano and a fiddle. Even the men at the bar were watching the show. Only a few of the tables were occupied by men more interested in draw poker than in women.

Doc Emory was seated at one of these tables, sullenly eying his poker hand. There was a bottle of whiskey on the table, more than half of it gone, and a whiskey glass at Doc's elbow.

Vickers felt a vague disquiet as he studied the man. Doc and Kip were the only two men in Fulton who knew who he was; in a way, his life was dependent on them.

He saw Kip as he crossed to the bar. Billens was sitting by himself under the flight of stairs leading to the upper floor. He had his chair tilted back against the wall. A cigarette was limp in the corner of his mouth; his hat was pulled low over his eyes. He had an unobstructed view of the front door and of the bar, but he did not seem to be particularly interested in anyone. If he saw Matt come in, he gave no indication of it.

A small frown cast a shadow of doubt across the U.S. marshal's face. Doc was unpredictable. But Kip Billens was like a rifle muzzle, as emotionless and as deadly.

Vickers found a hole in the bar line and waited for the busy bartender to attend to him. Next to him an unshaven, stumpy man in a red flannel shirt which obviously hadn't been washed in weeks was waving his dirty gray hat under his companion's nose. He jostled Matt, turned around and grinned triumphantly, eager to spill his grievances to a new audience.

He held up his hat and poked his finger through a ragged hole in the crown. "Twenty pesos, fella," he fumed. "Wore it less than five years, an' some dirty polecat puts a slug through it. Mindin' my own business, I was. An' some dirty polecat—"

His companion tried to silence him. But Flannel Shirt was grievously drunk. "Up by Indian Tanks I was, fella. I was mindin' my own business. Thought I'd take a look at the old Spanish diggin's before comin' back to town. That's when I saw this mirage—"

His slat-thin partner started to drag him away from the bar. "You've been swillin' enough rotgut to see a dozen mirages, Foley," he muttered. "Let's go home."

"Angel on a white hoss," Foley insisted. He pulled free of his companion's grasp. "Saw her plain as I see you." He focused his unsteady gaze on his partner. "Plainer—an' a danged sight prettier, too!" He hiccupped loudly. "Then some dirty polecat put this hole in my new hat!"

His companion brought up his long right arm, his fist smacking solidly against Foley's drooling jaw. Foley staggered. His partner caught him and held him upright. He turned and eyed Matt, his mouth twisting apologetically. "Foley sees things when he's drunk, fella. Don't mind him."

Matt watched them weave across the room toward the door. Behind him the bartender's voice barked, "What's yours, mister?"

"Whiskey," Matt said automatically, turning. He reached in his pocket as the man slopped liquor into a glass and pushed it toward him. Matt brought out the notched coin and placed it on the counter, his attention seemingly occupied with the dancing girls on the stage.

The bartender's eyes widened. He wiped his hands on his apron and hurriedly closed his fingers over the coin. "I'll get your change," he mumbled.

Vickers' glance followed him up a short flight of open stairs to a mahogany-railed balcony jutting into the room above the end of the bar. The bartender knocked lightly on the varnished door, then went inside.

Matt recalled the building's odd architecture—he guessed that the door gave access to the low, tacked-on wing.

His gaze came back across the crowded room; he noticed that Kip Billens had moved slightly. His hat was pushed up on his head. He was not looking at Matt.

The batwings banged against the wall as a hard-faced man came inside, a paper clenched in his right fist. He paused briefly, searching the room for someone, then walked directly to the table where Doc was playing in a four-handed game of poker. He tapped one of the players on the shoulder and dropped the paper down on the table in front of him, jabbing his forefinger to indicate something important in it.

Matt's glance narrowed on the card players. One was a thin man in shirt sleeves, smoking a thick black cigar, wearing a flat-crowned black hat pushed far back on his head, showing a receding hairline that emphasized a bulging forehead. Someone had once laid a white-hot poker across that forehead just above the eyes, and the flesh had crinkled and left a scarred welt which hung like ugly brows over pale, deadly eyes.

Matt had seen that face on several Wanted dodgers. Pip Raney, wanted in several towns up in Wyoming Territory. A gunman with a bad reputation.

Raney reached out and picked up the newspaper. He wadded it in his fist and tossed it aside. If what had been brought to his attention was supposed to mean something to him, it did not register on his face.

The man who had brought it to his attention scowled; he stepped away from the table and headed for the bar. He was a lean, hungry-looking kid with a tough sneer on his narrow face which had imprinted itself on his mean and insignificant soul.

He pushed up beside Vickers, gave Matt a level, belligerent stare, then pounded on the bar top for service.

The bartender was just coming through the hinged counter opening. He scurried up hastily and quickly set a bottle and a glass before the man.

Matt finished his drink and eyed the nervous bartender. "My change," he reminded him.

The bartender licked his lips. He made a slight

head motion toward the stairs.

Vickers turned, hooked his elbows on the bar and watched the girls. When they finished, they came down from the stage and started mingling with the customers, their laughter shrilling in the room.

Matt took the opportunity to move out of the bar line and head for the stairs. The tough kid at the counter watched him go; he gulped his drink and turned away, heading for the door.

Kip Billens came lazily to his feet and drifted outside after the kid.

Matt, mounting the stairs to the balcony, did not see them leave. Doc's lidded gaze had followed the movements of all three men; he looked across the table at Raney and licked dry, cottony lips.

Things were going wrong—all wrong!

Up on the balcony overhanging the bar, Matt was knocking on the door. A woman's low voice asked him to come in.

Vickers hesitated a moment; his glance went down to Doc Emory, but the man was studying his cards. Vickers could not see Kip's chair from where he stood.

He opened the door and stepped inside.

— IV —

THE WOMAN WAS standing by the window which faced the bridge and the dark gully separating her from the older section of Fulton. A china-based lamp was on a round table in the middle of the room, and its harsh glare did not reach her; the shadows were kind to her, softening the fleshy outlines of her body, masking the lines in her face.

She had been looking out of the window, but Vickers had the unaccountable feeling that she had not been noticing what lay below her, but had been staring inward into the bleakness of her thoughts.

She turned, and a ring on her finger sparkled brightly as she waved. She said, "Come in, come in." Her voice was low, almost masculine in its timbre.

Matt walked to the table. The notched coin lay on the fringed damask tablecloth.

"I'm Victoria Barnes," the woman said. "Professionally, it's Vicki." Her smile and her voice were matter-of-fact. "No one calls me Victoria any more."

The United States marshal waited. She moved away from the window, and the glare from the lamp defined her with pitiless accuracy. She was in her late forties, and once she must have been a striking woman; but the years had padded too well an already full figure, so that now she looked blowsy. Her auburn hair was streaked with gray.

She gestured to the coin on the table. "Is that yours?"

"I had it," Vickers admitted. He glanced around the room. It was furnished in a dark Victorian style. An open door gave him a glimpse of a four-poster bed, a small chiffonier.

"Then you received my note?" she asked. Her voice was a little impatient.

Matt shrugged. He could not shake off a feeling of uneasiness; he was not quite willing to commit himself.

She frowned. "I sent the United States marshal's office in Houston that coin and a note. The man who showed up here had to be—" She paused, her face whitening. Her eyes, a luminous violet, searched Matt's face with sudden desperate inquiry.

"You are from the marshal's office, aren't you? You were sent here?"

"I came on orders from Houston," Matt admitted.

Vicki Barnes licked her lips. "You're being overly cautious, then." She shrugged. "Perhaps you have a right to be. There was another lawman who came to Fulton. He didn't last long."

"Do you know who killed him?"

The woman hesitated. "No one saw it. But the word which came to me said it was Ret Blue. He's Luke McQuade's half-brother."

Matt nodded, his suspicions leaving him. He reached inside his pocket and tossed the note which had accompanied the coin on the table.

"You said in this you would tell me where the Marlowe women can be found. Who's holding them prisoner? Is it Luke McQuade?"

Vicki Barnes shook her head. In the momentary silence a board creaked inside the bedroom. She didn't hear it; she seemed to be regretting the decision which had prompted the letter to the

U.S. marshal's office.

"No, it isn't Luke." Her voice was strained. She turned away from Matt, looking out through the dark window. "Luke only took orders."

"Who is it then?"

She drew in a deep breath. "A man I once thought I would marry. A man I was madly in love with." Her voice was low, bleak with an old rancor. She moved away from the window; in the lamplight, her face was hard despite the sag of flesh under her chin.

Matt waited, sensing the growing indecision in her now, the clash of fear with a love that had turned to hate. Whoever the man was, he once had meant a lot to Victoria Barnes.

"Telling me who that man is might save us a lot of useless trouble, Miss Barnes," he pressed her gently.

She shook her head. "Tomorrow. After nine. I'll ride with you, Marshal. I'll show you where to find the Marlowe women—and the man you really want."

"I might not be around tomorrow," Matt said bluntly. "There's always that chance. Tell me now."

"Tomorrow." Her voice was stubborn. "I

want to be with you when you arrest him."

Matt gave in. "Tomorrow, then." He nodded briefly and turned to the door.

The woman slumped against the heavy table and watched the door close behind the tall U.S. marshal. She was seeing herself for what she was, and regretting what she might have been.

The voice from the bedroom made a cruel intrusion into her turbulent thoughts.

"You're wrong, Vicki! You won't ride with Matt Vickers tomorrow. You won't ride anywhere!"

She whirled, the soft flesh of her body quivering. Fear grayed her sagging features. "Who—how'd you get in here?"

The voice held a caustic quality. "Your back stairs. And a bedroom window, unlocked. I don't make much noise, coming or going—or killing!"

There was a gun in his hand and no pity in his eyes as he moved toward her. Terror knifed through the woman. She turned and stumbled against the table, and the lamp teetered perilously. Then she was around it, heading for the door, and a scream started up in her throat.

The man was after her like a cat. The flat side of his Colt came down in a cross-swipe against

her head, sending her sprawling across the bro-
cade-covered couch.

She did not lose consciousness. A groan slipped
from between her lips. She twisted around to
look up at him, her eyes wide and dark and
pleading.

The killer had holstered his Colt. He reached
over her for a fluffy fringed pillow and brought
it down over her face. He leaned his weight on it.

Vicki Barnes struggled weakly. The blow on
her head had dazed her. Her manicured fingers
came up instinctively to tear at the smothering pillow, at the man's iron hands. Her nails
clawed across the backs of his hands, and he
cursed her harshly but did not remove the pillow.

After a few moments Vicki's hands fell away.

He waited, counting methodically to himself.
Then he lifted the pillow from her face. Her
mouth was open, as if she had tried desperately,
and in vain, to suck in one last breath of air. He
lifted the back of his scratched hand, wetting it,
and held it close to her mouth. He sensed no
movement of air, no perceptible indication of
breathing. He checked her pulse. She was dead.

He left her sprawled across the couch, a leg
and one arm dangling grotesquely. He walked

swiftly to the door, slid the bolt into position, and retreated the way he had come. His passage through the bedroom window made no sound.

MATT VICKERS came down the stairs into the smoke-fogged barroom. The girls were on stage again, clustered coyly around a buxom redhead who was singing a naughty ballad about a cowboy, a ball of twine and a tryst behind a barn.

Doc was still playing cards with Raney; his eyes lifted to Matt, and he flashed the marshal a worried glance.

The singer had a husky, suggestive voice, and she was pleasing the customers, who whistled and stamped their feet in approval.

Matt paused on the last step and reached inside his pocket for the makings. He was thinking of the woman upstairs when Ret Blue shouldered through the saloon batwings.

Blue came into the bar looking for Vickers; there was a grim, unmistakable purpose in his movements. He had changed from his uncomfortable suit to a dark flannel shirt and gray trousers. A belt gun, bone-handled, rode on his right hip.

He saw Vickers almost at once and moved

aside quickly, his eyes narrowing in grim antici-
pation. Behind him Shorty pushed through the
saloon doors, followed by the tough kid who had
brought Raney the newspaper earlier. Shorty and
the kid separated, taking positions on either side
of the Pecos Bar door.

Most of the customers were watching the on-
stage show, but the few near the entrance caught
the impending violence foreshadowed on Ret's
dark face and glanced swiftly across the room
toward Matt Vickers.

Ret started toward the marshal, his stride short
and deliberate. His passage seemed to send rip-
ples of alarm ahead of him, so that men in his
path turned to see what was causing it.

Doc Emory froze. Raney was watching Ret,
frowning. The redheaded singer's throaty voice
sounded harsh in the rapidly growing stillness.

The U.S. marshal stood on the last step, knowing that there was no way of avoiding trouble,
knowing that Ret Blue would never overlook what
had happened inside the railroad depot.

The gunman's harsh voice confirmed his premonition. "I looked through half of Fulton for
you, mister!" he grated. "You should have left
town when I told you to!"

The buxom singer stopped in mid-ballad, and the girls stood around her, watching the center of attention shift from them to the tall man on the steps.

Raney scraped his chair back and stood up. Doc Emory sat very still, his cards crumpled in his left hand. His right hand rested in his lap. He didn't look up. He seemed to be staring moodily into his empty whiskey glass.

"What's up, Ret?" Raney's voice was sharp.

"Nothing I can't handle alone, Pip," Ret said contemptuously. "This joker stuck his nose into my private life. I'm gonna skin him for it!"

Vickers waited. He could take care of Ret, and possibly Shorty and the tough kid. He wouldn't have time for Raney. He flicked a glance toward the far stairs, looking for Kip Billens. But the brother of Sheriff Billens was gone.

His gaze swung back to Ret Blue; it glowed with a cold gray light. "You talk a lot," he said thinly. "It's gone to your head."

Ret sneered. "I'm gonna do more than just talk. I'm gonna pull you off that step and kick you clear across this room, unless you get up enough guts to make a try for that gun you're wearing?"

He was close by now, balanced and deadly. He reached out his left hand to Matt's coat, his right hand poised like a claw over his gun butt.

Vickers' right hand didn't drop to his holster. It flicked out eleven inches, caught Ret on the side of the jaw and twisted the gunman's head around in a lopsided position. His left hand came up with a Colt. Ret's knees were just beginning to buckle when Matt shot over him and hit Shorty, who was just beginning his draw.

Shorty fell back against the wall. His legs held him up, but he had lost interest in the fight.

The tough kid wasn't so lucky. Vickers' second slug glanced off his leveled Colt and caught him in the stomach.

Raney's fingers were gripped around his gun butt when Doc Emory's muzzle leveled across the table at him. Doc's voice was low. "Keep out of it, Pip!"

Raney let his hand fall away from his gun; he looked down at Doc, his yellowish eyes narrowing with quick understanding.

Ret was down on his hands and knees, shaking his dazed head. He looked up at Matt, his eyes clearing; he came to his feet then, his hand making another try for his gun.

Vickers kicked it out of his hand. The heavy Colt .44 skidded under a nearby table, and Ret's lips pulled back against his teeth as he hugged smashed fingers.

Matt took a step down toward him, and Ret lunged to meet him, swinging wildly. Vickers batted his fist aside and put his weight behind the gun muzzle he buried in Ret's stomach.

The gunman jackknifed, and Vickers cuffed him contemptuously, spinning him around and booting him away from the stairs.

Raney stood by and watched Ret Blue sprawl almost at his feet. His eyes held a cold surprise.

Matt laid his hard gaze on Raney. "Is he a friend of yours?"

Raney licked his lips; he shrugged.

"Don't make the same mistake he did," Matt warned him bluntly. "I didn't come in here looking for trouble. I could have killed him. Tell him that when he's up to listening again."

Raney nodded.

Matt walked to the door and waited there for Doc, who backed slowly across the silent room. They stepped outside into the night, the batwings creaking behind them.

There was no immediate stirring from the men

inside the Pecos Bar. Vickers holstered his gun and ducked under the tie-bar to his horse. His hand on the bit reins, he turned to Doc.

"Where's Kip?"

Doc Emory shook his head. "I don't know." His voice was strained, uneasy.

Matt scowled. He was sitting in the saddle when a shadow materialized out of the darkness. Kip's hard face showed briefly in a patch of light.

"Step out for a breath of air, and all hell breaks loose inside," he commented thinly. He sounded disappointed.

Matt swung his horse away from the rack as Kip mounted alongside. Doc kneed his gray mare beside them. "Where to, Matt?"

"The Standish House," Vickers replied. "We'll put up there for the night and see what develops in the morning."

Kip's laughter was short. "If I know anything about Luke McQuade, a lot will start developing —and fast!"

Matt eyed the younger man for a moment, then shrugged. "That's what we came after, isn't it?"

Kip nodded. "Yeah—I guess it is."

But Doc was looking at him with a strange bitterness in his eyes.

IT WAS A long while before Ret Blue was able to ride away from the Pecos Bar. He rode alone through a narrow, littered alley that took him to the east end of the town and onto a faint trail that led up to a small shack huddled in the darkness of a low hill.

Overhead, the moon was blotted out by a thickening haze. There was a dampness in the air that seemed to reach into Ret's bones.

He pulled up before the cabin and waited impatiently. Finally the door opened; he had no view of the man inside, who came to the doorway.

"Ret?"

The gunman nodded. "We've got trouble," he said harshly. "A big feller came to town tonight. He killed Pete an' put Shorty in bed with a busted shoulder."

Ret continued with a terse rundown on what had occurred in the Pecos Bar, not sparing himself.

But he tried to salvage his pride in conclusion. "I underestimated him tonight. I'll make sure of him next time. Thought you ought to know, though."

The voice from the cabin doorway had a bitter sting. "You poor fool! Next time he'll kill you.

That big fellow is Matt Vickers, a United States marshal."

Ret stiffened. "You sure?"

"Did I ever tell you anything I wasn't sure of?" The voice held a contemptuous rebuke.

Ret sucked in his dry lips. "Vickers, eh?"

"Stay away from him," the voice advised. "Leave Matt Vickers to your brother."

Ret's eyes glittered. "Luke's over at Track Town. I can handle this federal lawman."

"Leave him to Luke," the voice cut in harshly. "Don't let a false pride push you, Ret. And don't foul things up now!"

The door closed. Ret stared into the blackness, his eyes bright with cold anger. Then he swung away, heading back to Fulton.

– V –

THE STANDISH HOUSE was the oldest building in Fulton and the most pretentious. It had a dining room which was usually well filled at mealtimes. This morning only a few of the tables were occupied. A thin rain beat against the windows, steamed up and blurred by the warmth inside.

Vickers was about through with breakfast when Doc Emory came into the room and joined him. Doc and Kip had shared the same room. Matt had bunked alone.

Emory looked like a man who had spent a sleepless night. His face was drawn; his eyes had a tired, saddened glaze.

"Kip's still asleep," he volunteered, pulling out a chair and sitting across from Matt. He placed a paper in front of the U.S. marshal.

"Picked it up at the counter," he explained. "I thought you might be interested."

He pointed to an announcement which dominated the front page of the *Fulton Gazette* with its big black type.

WANTED
A TOWN MARSHAL FOR FULTON
No embarrassing questions asked.
State salary wanted. Contact John
Carlson, City Commissioner.

"Town must be getting desperate," Doc said, "to put an ad like that in the local paper." He took a small tin of snuff from his pocket and put a pinch in each nostril. He shook his head.

"You find out anything last night?"

Matt Vickers shrugged. "Not much. Just enough to convince me that Luke McQuade is taking orders from somebody else, not running the show himself." He frowned. "I never really believed he was bucking the Desert Line on his own, Doc. I just couldn't see what he had to gain out of wrecking the railroad."

"Who's hiring Luke?"

"I don't know. Not yet, anyway. But I expect to find out today, if she doesn't back out on me." He told Doc Emory about his meeting with Vickie

Barnes the night before.

Doc shook his head. "She sounds like a woman with an axe to grind." His eyes held a thin cynicism. "She could be a blind alley, Matt."

He broke off, his gaze caught by someone coming into the room behind Matt. He leaned back, his face tightening. His voice lowered.

"I think we're going to have company."

Matt turned his head. Two men had paused in the dining room entrance. One was a tall, gray-haired man with a neat, efficient look about him. He could have been a banker or a successful businessman. At the moment he looked worried. The man with him was short and square, with a broad, ruddy Irish face. He said something to the tall man as they crossed to Matt's table.

The rain lashing against the windows seemed to dampen any cheerfulness the few diners might have felt. The gray chill in the air cast a dismal silence over the tables.

The two men came over, and the tall man said, "Good morning, gentlemen," nodding to Matt and Doc. He had a pleasant voice. "I'm John Carlson." He inclined his head toward the newspaper in front of the U.S. marshal. "You've read my ad, I notice." He indicated the short man by his side. "This is George Melvin. He publishes the *Gazette*."

Matt Vickers waved to chairs. "Sit down." He did not introduce himself or Doc Emory.

The two men sat across the table from them. Carlson glanced briefly at Doc; then his attention centered on Matt. His voice was blunt. "George was in the Pecos Bar last night. He told me what happened."

Matt waited. Doc eased back in his chair, his eyes half closed.

"I'm asking you to consider seriously taking the job of town marshal," Carlson said. He stated the proposition hopefully.

Vickers frowned. He did not want to get involved in the town's troubles in this way; it wasn't what he was down there for.

"Why me?" he asked indifferently. "You don't know me."

The *Gazette* publisher chipped in; he had a rough, direct manner. "I saw how you handled Ret Blue last night. You killed Pete Silvers and put Shorty Falk out of commission. And you put the fear of God into Raney, too." He smiled. "For my money, mister, you're the man we want as town marshal."

Matt shook his head. "You're making a mistake. What happened last night doesn't prove I'll make a good lawman for you."

Carlson's spare features looked tired. "We're willing to take a chance you'll do a good job," he said. "There isn't anyone in town, or anywhere else that I know of, who's willing to buck Luke McQuade and his bunch of killers. I'll lay our cards on the table. The town's gone wild since Sheriff Tom Billens was killed. We tried to get another law officer. No one wants the job. We sent for Ranger help. They sent us a man named Rawlings. He was killed shortly after he arrived in town."

Carlson made a weary gesture. "It's not only because of the trouble in town that I'm concerned. So far Luke has kept his boys pretty quiet here. But someone's trying to wreck the railroad. Two trains have been dynamited within the past month. Fulton needs that railroad. If it folds up, a lot of this town will go broke with it."

Matt studied the man for a moment. "Do you think Luke McQuade is trying to break the railroad?"

Carlson shrugged. George Melvin sneered. "You won't find any witness with guts enough to say so. But the trouble started right after Luke and his bunch came to town. Tom was a good lawman, and not afraid of the devil himself. But they killed him. No one saw them string him up, except maybe Bevans. But he's dead, too. The next night Frank Wilson, Tom's deputy, was hauled into an alley and badly beaten. When he recovered, he left town."

Matt shook his head; he still did not want to get tied up in this as a town officer.

"I'm sorry," he said evenly. "But what makes you folks think I can do what Sheriff Billens couldn't?"

Melvin plucked at his square jaw. "I saw you in action last night," he repeated. "Besides," he added grimly, "you haven't got much choice. After what happened, you'll either have to leave town or buck Luke McQuade. You won't be left alone, that's for sure."

Vickers nodded slowly. What the newspaper publisher was saying was true. He glanced across the table at Doc, and beyond the small quiet man he saw Kip Billens come to the entrance of the dining room, pause briefly as he saw the two men at the table with Vickers, then move toward them.

A strange impulse made the U.S. marshal say,

"I can't accept your offer, gentlemen, for reasons of my own. But would Sheriff Billens' brother do?"

Carlson frowned. "Brother? I didn't know Tom had a brother."

Doc Emory put in sharply, "Long as you're holding out that job offer, gentlemen, let me put in my bid for it."

Matt swung a quick frowning glance at him. But Doc was looking off toward Kip; he didn't notice.

Kip Billens came up to the table and looked down at Doc. For once he did not have a cigarette dangling between his lips. He asked lightly: "Take what job, Doc?"

"Town marshal," the small man said. He looked at Carlson, then at the publisher, Melvin. "I was in on what happened at the Pecos Bar last night," he reminded them. "What applies to my friend here goes for me, too. And I'm not planning to leave town."

Carlson hesitated. Melvin was disappointed and made no attempt to hide it.

"I'm not as handy with a gun as Matt," Doc continued, glancing at Vickers. "But my partner here—" he indicated Kip with a wave of his hand—"will back me up. Won't you, Kip?"

Kip licked his lips like a baffled cat. "Yeah, I'll back you, Doc. But I think you're a darn fool to take the job."

Carlson rose. "Well, if you'll come around to the sheriff's office in about a half-hour, I'll swear you in and give you Tom's badge." He looked at Vickers. "Are you planning to stay on in town?"

Vickers nodded. "For a while."

Melvin stood up beside Carlson. "I don't know what caused the trouble between you and Ret," he said grimly, "and as far as I know you may be just another fast gun with a grudge against Luke McQuade's bunch. But if I were you, I'd keep away from dark alleys from now on."

He waved briefly and joined Carlson on the way out.

Kip Billens eased his hard frame into a chair across from the U.S. marshal. He was wearing an unbuttoned brush jacket over his faded range clothes, and the brass shell casings filling the loops of his cartridge belt gleamed coldly. A pair of skin-tight gloves covered his hands.

His eyes held a curious glitter as he looked at Emory. "You serious about this, Doc?"

Emory kept his eyes on his coffee cup. It

seemed to Matt that Doc was holding something
back, something that was weighing on him. Again
an uncertainty about the two men nagged at the
U.S. marshal. Doc and Kip Billens seemed to
have tensions and complexities of their own which
he could not understand.

"It'll feel good wearing a star again," Doc
said finally. "I don't intend to let this one down."
His glance came up, and he regarded the younger
man, who was smiling thinly. "You came here
to even things for your brother," he said quietly.
"I'd appreciate your backing me, son."

A flicker of uncertainty came into Kip's eyes;
a muscle twitched in his cheek. It was the only
time Matt had seen any emotion in the man.

"Sure," Kip answered colorlessly, "if that's
what you want."

Matt scraped back his chair and stood up. "I'm
with you, Doc. You know that. We're in this together. But I've got a call to make. When I get
back, we'll know who we're bucking here, besides Luke McQuade."

Doc nodded. "I'll be in the sheriff's office,
Matt." He watched the tall marshal move away.
He was silent a long time; then he turned to Kip,
who was eying him with impassive coldness.

"We told him we'd back him up," Doc said slowly, tightly, through his teeth. "Let's not let him down, eh, kid?"

He made it a question, his eyes searching the younger man's face. He saw nothing there to reassure him. Inside himself he felt sick; in the emptiness of his hopes, his own bitter voice mocked him. *"What do you expect? You can't undo what's done, Doc—a man never can!"*

MATT VICKERS rode his roan horse out of the hotel stable, ducking his head against the thin, driving rain. In the street he met Doctor Blake, driving a buggy, heading out of town. The young doctor waved and pulled up, and Matt rode alongside.

"How's Mr. Grover?" Matt asked.

"Fine," Doctor Blake answered professionally. "His job gives him a worse headache than his injury." He hesitated. "I heard what happened last night. I patched up Shorty's shoulder." He leaned forward, his eyes showing worry. "I wish it had been Ret Blue you killed, Matt."

Vickers shrugged. "He won't be bothering Betty for a while," he answered casually.

A trace of resentment came into the young

doctor's face at this; he answered stiffly, "That's what she said last night, after you had gone. I wish I could feel the same way about him. But I don't even know who you are, or what has brought you to Fulton. For all I know, you might he just another tough with a quick gun. However, Betty seems to feel she can trust you." He reddened, his voice coming out now in a quick harsh rush. "As a matter of fact, she seems to have fallen in love with you! And I can't say that I blame her. This is a rough town, and she needs protection. Her father is too old, and I'm—"

"You'll do," Matt cut in quickly. "I wouldn't worry about Betty. And if it'll ease your mind any, I'm here on business that will help the railroad and the Grovers, too."

Young Blake settled back. "It makes me feel better hearing you say it," he admitted. He picked up the reins. "I'm driving out to Track Town— part of my job. Oh, by the way, do you know Chris Marlowe?"

"Why?"

"Saw someone in town this morning who looked like him." Blake shook his head. "Couldn't be, though." He smiled. "Betty invited you over for supper tonight. The Grovers live in a cottage on Flint Street, a white house under a big cotton-wood." His voice was without resentment now.

Matt waved briefly and watched the buggy wheels stir up the puddles in the street. He puzzled over Blake's remark. If Marlowe was in town, he'd be showing up at the depot, or trying to get in touch with Paul Grover, surely.

The buildings flanking the road dripped in the morning rain, looking dingy and uncomfortable under the gray sky. Matt turned his thoughts to Vicki Barnes. It was a bad day to go riding. Would she try to put him off again?

The roan's hoofs pounded on the wooden planks. Matt's glance roved along the building line. There was little morning traffic. But he remained alert, knowing that what had occurred last night had been a gauntlet thrown in the face of the McQuade crowd; he knew they would not let it stand that way.

No one appeared to challenge him. Vickers pulled his roan up by the empty rack of the Pecos Bar. The heavy inside door was closed against the batwings. Evidently the bar did not open in the morning.

Vickers walked up the steps and knocked on the downstairs door. He listened to the faint re-

verberations of his fist on the other side of the
heavy panel. He tried once more and was about
to turn to the outside wing stairway when he
heard footsteps inside the bar come toward him.
A moment later a heavy bolt drew back, and a
beard-stubbled, suspicious-looking face peered
out at him. The man was holding a mop handle
in his hands.

"Yeah?"

Matt pushed the door open and walked inside.
"I came to see Miss Barnes. Is she up?"

"Eh?"

Matt repeated the question, frowning a little.
The swamper turned and stared doubtfully toward
the door to Vicki's apartment. "Didn't see her
this morning. She always sleeps late." His voice
was a grumble. "I just work here."

Matt glanced about the empty barroom with
its chairs and tables stacked against the walls.
Stale tobacco smoke lingered in the dimly lighted
room. The building was very quiet.

A black and white tomcat with a blue ribbon
tied neatly around his neck came padding noise-
lessly down the stairs from the upper floor. He
came across the room to rub his whiskers against
Matt's legs.

The swamper cursed and shook his mop at the cat. "Scat, blast you!" he growled. "Can't stand cats," he muttered. It was not an apology.

The cat jumped up on the bar and went down out of sight behind it.

Matt ignored the swamper and went up the steps to Vicki's apartment. He rapped sharply on the door.

He received no answer, nor did he hear the slightest movement from beyond the closed door. He recalled then that the bedroom was at the far end of the apartment and rapped louder.

The swamper remained in the middle of the barroom, leaning on his mop handle, scowling.

Matt banged once more. The silence beyond the door had a quality that raised the hackles on his neck; a feeling that something was wrong inside the apartment grew in him. He tried the doorknob and discovered that the door was locked. He leaned his shoulder against it and found its heavy panels unyielding. It would take a lot of battering to break it in.

The marshal walked back down the stairs and across the empty barroom to the front door. The swamper watched him leave without comment.

Outside, Matt hesitated. It was quite likely that

Vicki Barnes had changed her mind. But he had to make certain.

He walked around to the back of the building. Rain dripped down from the eaves, splattering on his hat. Some of it seeped down his neck.

He found a flight of outside stairs along the side of the wing; they led up to a small landing protected from the weather by a wooden awning.

The door was locked. Baffled, Matt knocked again, several times, before he decided that if the Barnes woman was inside, she was not going to answer.

He was turning away when the window just off the landing caught his attention. Matt straddled the shaking railing and pressed close to the window, wiping away rain streaks in order to have a clearer view inside.

He could see the bed, most of it, and the wardrobe across the room. He could make out that the bed had not been slept in.

Aroused now, and alerted, he tried the window. It went up easily, quietly. Matt slid his leg across the sill and ducked inside.

Out in the street in front of the Pecos Bar, two men paused briefly, glancing up at the wing landing.

"That was Vickers!" Ret Blue breathed sharply. "We've got him cold this time, Raney, the way we want him. Breaking and entering!"

Raney nodded. "I'll follow him up the stairs, Ret." He eased along the building side, his Colt in his hand.

Ret pushed open the front door and stepped quickly inside, gun in hand. He kicked the door shut and whirled to face the swamper, who had jerked around and was staring goggle-eyed at him.

Ret's voice was a deadly whisper. "Get out of here pronto, Pop!"

The swamper dropped his mop and sidled quickly to the door. Ret bolted it behind him. His smile was as vicious as a tiger's as he wheeled about and stalked across the room to the stairs leading up to Vicki Barnes' apartment.

– VI –

MATT VICKERS paused inside Vicki's bedroom. The faint odor of perfume was an intimate
thing in the room. His glance passed quickly over
its details. The bed had not been slept in, but
there were clothes strewn about and hanging in
the closet, which precluded the notion that Vicki
Barnes had decided to leave Fulton after talking
with him.

He passed through the bedroom into the living
room and saw at once why the woman had not
answered his knock. Even before he bent over and
examined her, Matt knew that Vicki Barnes was
dead.

She had stiffened overnight into a grotesque
position. Her trailing arm was rigid. Her face was
a mask fashioned with a faint hint of terror, deftly
brought out by the wide, staring eyes.

Matt found a bruise under the mass of hair on the left side of her head, but he knew it was not this blow that had killed her. There was that in her features which suggested strangulation, yet there were no marks of strong fingers around her throat. In fact, there was no sign of violence on Vicki other than the small bruise hidden by her hair.

Matt looked down at her fingers, curled and set by death. Dark brown flecks tinged her nails; one of them was broken off. Matt's attention was caught by the pillow next to her head, and he had a sudden gruesome insight into how Vicki Barnes had died.

It must have happened almost immediately after he had left her, he thought grimly—the killer must have been waiting in the bedroom, listening while she talked to him.

Vickers straightened, feeling a momentary sense of futility. She had been afraid last night, but bitterly defiant—and now she was dead. He wondered why she had been willing to tell him who was behind the trouble here. There had been something in her voice when she had spoken of the man, a familiarity that hinted at some previous intimacy.

The thought came to Matt Vickers that now he would probably never know, unless there was something in the room—some letters perhaps—that would tell him what Vicki Barnes no longer could.

He was starting to turn toward the small desk across the room when he heard a faint sound inside the bedroom. He went alert, listening. It had sounded like a boot scraping across the window sill. But the burst of rain slamming into the windows blotted it out before he grasped hold of it.

The U.S. marshal listened tensely, but the sound was not repeated, nor did he hear anything else. He walked to the table where he had left the coin and Vicki's note the previous night; they were still there, and he pocketed them. He noticed that the chimney lamp was black with soot, and he surmised the flame must have turned smoky just before the last of the coal oil burned itself out.

Vickers turned to the small desk and saw that the drawer had been pulled out. Papers and letters were on the desk top, hastily pawed through. If there had been anything there to give him a clue, it was now gone. Matt started to close the drawer, and now he heard a faint step from the bedroom and knew instantly that he was being watched. He felt the small hair on the back of his neck stand up.

He moved on impulse then. He turned to the door leading down to the barroom below and drew back the bolt; he pulled the door open and then spun back, away from it, drawing and whirling to face the bedroom door.

Raney loomed up, stepping quickly, his gun leveled. He jerked around to follow Matt's movements, his gun muzzle trying to target the U.S. marshal. He fired once, his bullet gouging into the wall behind Matt.

Vickers' gun blasted twice, and Raney spun around and fell.

The gunshots bounced back from the hemming walls and faded slowly. In the trembling, shocked silence, the rain seemed to whimper against the streaked windows.

Matt moved with quick strides, stepping over Raney's body, and glanced into the bedroom. He saw no one else, nor was there any other movement save that of the curtains at the open window through which Luke McQuade's gunman had evidently followed him.

It was quiet in that section of the building, but

from the upper floor he could hear movement and what seemed to be the muted cries of women, and then he remembered that the Pecos Bar entertainers lived there.

There was nothing more he could do there, Matt thought bleakly, and he had no desire to confront frightened, questioning women.

He walked quickly back to the door leading down to the barroom and stepped out onto the balcony. He still had his cocked gun in his hand, and he paused briefly by the railing to glance down into the dimly lighted room below.

Down and off to Matt's left, a cat screamed in sudden outraged pain, and Matt whirled to face the sound.

Ret Blue's first shot, flung wild because of the unexpected caterwauling underfoot, splintered wood three feet above Matt's head. A strangled, surprised curse broke from the gunman. He had not noticed Vicki's cat, which had come up from somewhere below to rub herself playfully against his legs; he had shifted slightly as Matt appeared on the balcony and had unknowingly trod on the feline's tail.

The advantage of surprise was gone now; Blue was thumbing back the hammer of his gun again when a red flare lanced down at him from the balcony.

Vickers' slug spun Ret around. He managed to get off another shot as he steadied himself against the bar and thought he saw Matt jerk back just as the marshal fired again. The bullet gouged across Ret's upper arm, but he was falling anyway, and he scarcely felt the pain.

Slowly, alertly, Matt came down the stairs. His restless glance probed the big, silent room, his gun cocked, ready. There was no one else in the Pecos Bar. Even the cat was gone, having streaked up the stairs to Vicki's apartment. But the women's voices, momentarily hushed by the gunfire, broke forth again, more audible now as they drifted down the stairs from the upper rooms.

Matt crossed swiftly to the barred front door, unbolted it and stepped out into the driving rain. From the doorway across the street the swamper saw him leave, saw him mount the big roan which had waited patiently for Matt at the tie-rack.

Man and horse swung away and went galloping back across the plank bridge to the older section of Fulton.

The swamper waited a few moments longer,

then straggled across the muddy street, followed by curious citizens attracted by the morning gun-fire. He entered the barroom just as the first girls came cautiously down the stairs, most of them still clad in wool wrappers, sleepy-faced, un-painted, unbeautiful.

He saw Ret Blue's body by the bar. . . . Even as he came into the room Ret moved; he struggled weakly to get to his feet. The man's gaze steadied on one of the girls who came up to help.

"Milly," Ret said raggedly, "get Red. . . . Get—" He trailed off, slipping away from her, sliding down into unconsciousness again.

Milly looked around uncertainly. The swamp-er, sensing a chance for a quick buck, turned and slipped out, unnoticed, into the rain.

DOC EMORY raised his right hand and was sworn in by John Carlson in the office which had been occupied by the late Sheriff Tom Billens. No one had been inside since the night his deputy had been badly beaten. Dust had laid a thin patina of disuse over everything. There was a close and musty smell in the dingy room. The rear of the big house was partitioned off into two cells. The doors of both were open, as though in mute acceptance of the law's demise in Fulton.

George Melvin was there with Carlson. There were several other grave-faced citizens who seemed oddly uneasy about the whole thing, who appeared to lack Carlson's confidence in this new move to restore some semblance of law and order in the town.

In the rain outside, a group of curious spectators were clustered around the door. Some of them were offering whispered bets as to how long the new town marshal would last.

Doc looked at the star Carlson pinned on his coat. His glance came up, and he caught the thin sneer on Kip's face before it faded.

Carlson said kindly, "At the moment there isn't enough money in Fulton to pay for what you're being asked to do, Emory."

He paused, eying the small, tired-faced man by the desk. His gaze moved to the taller, sandy-stubbled figure by the cells, standing aloof, relaxed, eying the ceremony with barely concealed cynicism. A feeling of uneasiness came to John Carlson, leaving him unsure about what he had done.

Doc answered him, "I applied for the job, didn't I?" His voice was devoid of feeling; it merely sounded tired.

Carlson shrugged. "You understand that the job is temporary," he began.

Melvin pushed up to Carlson's side, saying, "Let's put it on the line, John; we owe him that much." He turned to Emory. "The job of sheriff in this county is an elective office. We tried holding an election right after Tom Billens was killed.

We offered twice the salary Tom received." He smiled bitterly. "No one tried for the job; no one will try, as long as Luke McQuade is in town. You know that, don't you?"

"I know," Doc said quietly.

Carlson took a deep breath. "About your salary—" he said slowly.

"Just pay me what you think I'm worth," Emory cut in sharply. There was impatience in him now; he was anxious to see them leave.

Carlson nodded. "If we can be of any help— I mean, if you find you need backing later on—" He trailed off, coloring a little.

He was asking this small man to face Luke McQuade's guns, and the only backing they would be able to give him would be verbal. Small consolation, he knew, and he saw an acknowledgement of this in Doc's faded eyes.

Carlson turned away then, leaving the office and taking the others with him. Doc followed them to the door and closed it behind them; he turned slowly and faced Kip Billens.

"Where were you last night?" His voice was grim.

Kip moved a shoulder lazily in partial reply. "Outside, waiting."

"Waiting for what?"

Kip didn't answer; his smile was enigmatic, aloof.

Doc Emory's voice held a raw, biting suspicion. "We rode into Fulton with Matt Vickers because that is the way you wanted it. You came to see me in Paseo, knowing that Vickers would be coming through there on his way here. You had never come to see me before—not in all those long years."

He choked back the hurt bitterness that rose achingly into his throat and waited a moment, getting back his control. Then, "You must have known even before I did that Marshal Vickers was coming to Fulton, didn't you?"

"I told you I did," Kip replied. His voice was colorless; he lounged against the cell bars, a hard, lazily balanced man, completely sure of himself.

"You told me a smooth story," Doc snapped back angrily. "Because you are who you are, I believed you. I wanted to believe you. So I lied and told Matt you were Tom Billens' brother, so that he would see nothing unreasonable in your coming here. We were friends—he *trusted* me!"

Emory sucked in a thin, angry breath. "Now I don't know any more. I don't know why you wanted to come here!"

He walked over to the younger man, his eyes dark, tortured by some inner guilt. "Just what are you after, Lou?"

The youngster said coolly, "Kip, Doc. Just call me Kip."

"What are you after?" Doc repeated grimly.

Kip straightened. For just an instant his eyes revealed a stark, uncompromising hatred of the small man. Emory saw it and stepped back, repelled by it.

"I told you in Paseo," Kip replied easily. His voice was colorless again. He knew Doc understood he was lying, and he didn't give a hoot. "I wanted to help you, that's all."

He shifted his attention from the small man as the office door opened; he stiffened slightly, alert now, his smile thin and cold.

Doc turned around, frowning.

Matt Vickers came inside, shoving the door closed behind him. There was a tear in his coat sleeve high above the elbow. Blood made a darker stain than the rain below the tear.

He eyed Kip and Doc for a moment, a smile twisting his lips wryly. "Badge looks good on you, Doc," he said. His glance shifted back to Kip. "Where's yours?"

Kip shrugged. "I don't need a badge to buck

the men who killed my brother." His eyes were hard on Matt's face, watching. "I didn't want to take their money under false pretenses."

Emory stepped up between them then; he eyed the blood on Matt's arm. "I see you ran into trouble."

The U.S. marshal nodded. He was preoccupied, his face dark and impassive. For the moment he was less concerned with the pain of the bullet wound than with what he had run into in the Pecos Bar.

"I ran into more than trouble," he growled. "I ran into a blank wall."

Emory studied Matt. "She run out on you?"

Vickers shook his head. "She's dead." He walked to the middle of the office and appraised it absently. "Someone smothered her to death with a pillow right after I left her last night."

Emory stared at him. Kip came away from the cell bars. His right thumb was hooked casually in his cartridge belt. He was still wearing his skin-tight black gloves.

He said, "What's all this about somebody getting smothered to death with a pillow, Matt?"

Matt looked at him, remembering now that he had not told Kip about his meeting with Vicki Barnes. He filled in the details now, mentioning his receipt of the notched coin and the subsequent events of the morning.

"I guess I was pretty lucky," he muttered. "If Ret hadn't stepped on that cat, I wouldn't be here now."

Kip whistled softly. "So you got Raney and Ret? When Luke gets this news, he'll come fogging into town looking for you, Matt!"

Matt frowned. "Raney was dead. I'm not sure about Ret." He shrugged. "I didn't wait to find out."

He looked at Kip. "I'll worry about Luke when I see him," he muttered. "The man I'm after is Luke's boss—the man Vicki Barnes was going to lead me to."

"You think he got wind of it and killed her?" Doc asked.

"It's a good guess," Matt agreed. "But it could have been someone else." He shook his head, baffled.

Kip made an offhand gesture. "Maybe there ain't any man behind Luke McQuade," he suggested. "From what I hear, Luke bosses his own shows. He gives orders; doesn't take them." He glanced off at the rain drumming on the window. "Maybe this woman was just trying to lead you away from here, away from Luke and the bunch who really run this town."

Matt shook his head. "I don't think so. Someone overheard us talking last night; he could have slipped into her bedroom from the outside landing, like I did this morning. It wasn't Ret and it wasn't Raney, and I know that Luke isn't in town. But whoever it was killed her to keep her from talking to me this morning."

He turned to Doc Emory. "You're the law here now, Doc. And it won't take long for word to get back across the bridge. You're going to have trouble. They know you were with me coming into town; you'll be the first man they'll hit, Doc."

Doc nodded stiffly. "I came to help out, Matt. And I knew what to expect when I asked for this star."

Matt nodded. "I'm glad you came along, Doc." He turned to face Kip. "This is what you said you wanted too, didn't you? The McQuade bunch killed your brother. Are you staying with Doc here?"

"You couldn't run me out of this town with a Gatling gun at my back," Kip said coldly. "I said I wanted in on this; I'm sticking!"

Matt smiled. "Well, that makes me feel better about leaving, Doc."

Kip's eyes held a flicker of surprise. "You going somewhere?"

Matt nodded. "I've got a couple of calls to make, and one of them may take me out of town."

"Want me to ride with you?" Kip asked.

Matt shook his head. "Luke will probably be in town before I get back. He may come here looking for me."

Doc said quietly, "I'll be waiting for him, Matt."

Matt shook his head again. "Don't meet him alone, Doc. He's fast." He put a hand on Doc's arm. "I don't want to lose you."

Doc pointed to Matt's wounded arm. "You better get that looked at," he said quietly. "Ain't there a doctor in town?"

"Doctor Blake," Matt said. "But he's gone up to Track Town."

"Then let me take a look at it," Doc insisted. "No sense running a risk of infection." He turned to Kip. "Get a bottle of whiskey," he ordered sharply, "somewhere—anywhere."

He looked at Matt as Kip went out. "It'll burn," he said, smiling a little, "but it's the best and quickest antiseptic at hand."

Kip came back with a small bottle as Doc was working on the gash on Matt's upper arm. The blood was beginning to congeal around the bullet cut.

"Clench your fist hard," Doc instructed Matt. As Matt did so, he asked: "Hurt?"

Matt shrugged. "I've had worse."

"Lucky," Doc said. "No torn nerves, no bones smashed."

He uncorked the bottle, held Matt's arm tightly and poured some of the whiskey into the cut. Matt jerked slightly, grinding his teeth against the fiery pain.

"Thanks, Doc," he grated.

Kip watched, poker-faced, as Doc bandaged Matt's arm. "Good thing you're not left-handed—your gun hand, I mean."

Matt slid his palm down over the butt of his holstered gun. 'Yeah," he said quietly, and helped Doc pull the sleeve down over the bandage on his left arm.

He looked at Kip, then back to Doc Emory. "I'll try to get back as soon as I can," he said. He walked to the door and paused; some premonition of disaster made him turn and say, "Good luck, Doc."

Then he stepped outside and was gone.

Doc remained by the desk, looking at the door. Kip shuffled his feet restlessly, eying Doc; then he turned and headed for the door.

Doc took a step after him. "No, Lou," he said grimly. "No."

Kip paused. He turned around, held by the sharp note of finality in Doc's voice. He said coldly, rebelliously, "I'm going out!"

Emory shook his head. His hand went up to brush the badge pinned to his coat, then slipped inside to his shoulder holster. His gun stopped Kip.

"No," he repeated bleakly. "You're staying here with me. We're waiting for Luke McQuade together, the way you told me you wanted it. Remember?"

Kip's hands tightened at his sides. He eyed Doc with bitter impatience; then a small smile erased the harshness from around his mouth.

He made a gesture with his hands. "All right, Doc," he said. "I was just going out to get something to eat." He started to walk toward Emory. "You wouldn't use that gun on me, now would you?"

Doc eyed him uncertainly. "If I have to," he said bitterly.

"You know I wouldn't let you face Luke alone," Kip said. He paused and sucked in a slow breath. "Maybe you and I have a lot of things to think over, things to forget. But if it came to a choice between you and Luke—" He put a hand on Doc's shoulder. "Now come on, Doc—trust me. For once in your life, trust me?"

Doc struggled against the doubts inside him. His eyes searched Kip's face. He wanted to believe this man; he *needed* to believe in him.

"Just this once, Lou," he whispered. "Just this once."

He slid his gun back inside his shoulder holster. "We'll back up Matt together?"

"To hell with Matt Vickers!" Kip said thinly. "I'm not doing this for him." He jerked a thumb toward the door. "Come on. I'll buy your dinner, Doc."

Doc's eyes darkened. "Lou—" His voice choked slightly. "Lou, I always wanted this. You and me—" His fingers tightened on Kip's arm.

"The best and biggest steak they serve, Lou." Doc was turning to the door as he talked, his eyes wet with an inner upheaval of emotion. He didn't see Kip's hand come up with his gun nestled flat in his palm; only at the last instant did he catch a glimpse of it. And by then it was too late!

— VIII —

PAUL GROVER stood on the platform, letting his thoughts run along the wet rails leading west into the rain-misted distance. Track Town lay fourteen miles in that direction, beyond the low hills that were gray ghosts against the dismal sky.

Betty was in the office, making entries in the ledger. He felt better with her near him. After last night he was keyed to trouble; he had promised himself he would not be caught off guard with Ret again.

He saw the horseman loom up out of the rain— a tall broad-shouldered figure on a mettlesome horse. Some of Paul's worries left him as he recognized Matt. He turned and walked the length of the platform to meet him.

Vickers dismounted, led his roan to the lee of the station and ground-reined him. He came up to the platform, his eyes studying Paul.

"Something I want to ask you," he said. "You busy?"

Paul waved. "Not that busy. Come on inside."

As they walked to the door together, Paul added trenchantly: "Even the weather's turned sour. Keeps up, there won't be a mile of track laid past Track Town, Luke McQuade or no Luke!"

Betty Grover put aside her ledger and came to her feet as Matt and her father entered the station office. Her smile of welcome was quick, friendly. "Good morning, Matt," she sang out.

Matt took off his hat and smiled a greeting. Then he saw a rifle, new and shiny, propped against the wall by the door, and he turned and eyed the station agent thoughtfully.

Paul Grover said defensively: "Just in case—"

"You won't need it," Matt interrupted bluntly. "Ret won't be back to bother your daughter."

Grover's eyes searched Matt's face. Betty came up to the railing, concern quickening her step. She noticed the tear in Matt's coat, the dark stain of blood. She opened the small door in the railing and came quickly to him.

"Matt," she said sharply, "did Ret—?" She

looked at him, waiting, a dark fear in her eyes.

"He tried to kill me," Matt said. "I shot him."

Paul Grover was more practical than his daughter. "Is he dead?"

Matt shrugged. "I don't know." He glanced at Betty. "But he won't be bothering you, not for quite some time, anyway."

She reached out and touched his arm. "You are hurt," she said softly.

"You can't ride around like that," Paul said. "I'll send someone to fetch Doctor Blake."

"He isn't in town," Matt told him. "Met him this morning; he was driving out to Track Town."

"I'll take care of it," Betty said. "We keep bandages and some antiseptic here for emergencies." She was turning, moving toward a small wall cupboard as she talked. "Dad, help him take off his coat."

Matt interrupted. "You won't have to, Miss Grover." She turned back to look at him, and he smiled at her. "Thanks anyway. But it wasn't much of a cut, and Doc Emory bandaged it for me."

"Doc Emory?" Betty looked at her father, who shrugged.

"A friend of mine," Matt explained. "We came to Fulton together."

"Oh!" Betty's voice held a mild disappointment.

"Next time I get hurt I'll come to you," Matt promised. He meant it as a compliment, and Betty Grover blushed.

"A woman likes to feel she's needed," she said, "especially by a man she likes." She was looking at Vickers with her face uplifted to his, and in that moment he saw her question and then accept him. She was his if he wanted her, and in that moment Matt Vickers felt the sharp loneliness of his job.

He said quietly, "I'm sure that Roger Blake needs you."

Betty Grover's eyes darkened. "Roger?" Then, catching herself, hurt, she forced a smile to her lips. "Roger is quite capable of taking care of himself."

Matt mentally cursed himself. He hadn't wanted to hurt this girl. But she scarcely knew him. And he couldn't get tied up, not a man with his short term life expectancy. It wouldn't be fair to her.

He murmured, "I didn't mean it that way. But

I thought that you and Doctor Blake—"

Behind them Paul Grover coughed discreetly.

Matt turned to him, glad of the interruption. "I really came to see you about sending out a wire for me, Mr. Grover."

The station agent nodded. "Fred usually handles the key. But I like to keep my hand in. Started out as a telegrapher myself, years ago."

He walked over to the telegraph key, settled himself in a chair, got his hand on the key and opened the wire. He looked up at Matt. "You want to write it down, or do you want to dictate it to me?"

Matt said, "I'll dictate it."

"Who are you sending it to?"

"Regional office, U.S. marshal, Austin."

Paul's head jerked up, his eyes widening.

"Ready?"

Grover nodded slowly and turned back to the key.

"Need urgent information," Matt dictated. "Did Tom Billens have a brother? If so, his name, general description, whereabouts?"

Grover worked the key. The clicking made a lonely, urgent sound in the small station. Paul's daughter stared at Matt, her eyes questioning, puzzled.

Grover was still tapping out the message when Matt added: "Find out if Chris Marlowe is still in Austin."

Grover looked up at him. "What?"

"Send it," Matt requested. "Just something that occurred to me. If Marlowe's still in Austin, I want to check out something with him."

Paul turned back to the key. "I see," he muttered. He finished the message, listening to the answering clicks of acknowledgement. He signed off, then turned back to the tall man standing over him.

"Where will I get in touch with you?"

"I'll drop by later today," Vickers answered. He started to swing away, paused. "Oh, one other thing, Mr. Grover. There were two men I ran into last night in the Pecos Bar." He described them as well as he could remember. "Foley was the name of the short one, the one with the bullet hole in his hat. He called his partner Joe. Know them?"

Paul Grover nodded. "That would be Bert Foley and Joe Ivers. Prospectors—the dry hole type. They've got a shack outside of town, about four miles west of here." He added directions.

Matt said, "Thank you, Mr. Grover."

"The name is Paul," the older man interrupted. "And if I can be of any further assistance—"

Matt shook his head. "I don't want you to get involved with my troubles, Paul. I shot Ret, and I imagine his brother Luke will want to see me about it. I don't want to see you or your daughter get mixed up in this. My shooting Ret had nothing to do with what happened here the other night."

Betty Grover came up to him, showing concern. "You will be back tonight?"

He shrugged. "I expect to be. But I have some pressing business, and I'll have to pass up that supper invitation, Miss Grover."

He touched his hat to her and turned away. Paul and Betty watched him go out into the rain; then, as her father turned to her, Betty whirled away from the small desk and went back to her ledger, slamming the small gate behind her.

There were tears in her eyes she didn't want her father to notice.

IX

VICKI BARNES' body had been removed from her apartment; so had that of Raney. Ret Blue lay on the woman's bed, his blood staining her counterpane. Since he was badly hurt, it had not seemed wise to move Ret further. He lay back now, his eyes closed, breathing with a painful effort.

Around him were clustered the house girls, inadequate in this emergency and concealing their indifference to Ret's condition behind masks of concern. It was not Ret they feared, but Luke McQuade. And Luke was due back soon.

Red Slater, one of McQuade's riders, glanced up from Ret to a lanky, poker-faced man coming into the room. Slim Favor had been sent out to bring Doctor Blake back to tend Ret. Red's eyes questioned the lanky long-rider.

Slim shook his head. "Doc must have gone out

of town on a call," he said. His voice lowered. "How is he?"

Red shrugged. Ret was conscious, despite the fact that he kept his eyes closed. He was weak, and he seemed to be running a fever. Inwardly Red cursed his own predicament. Ret had sent for him, thereby placing the responsibility for him on Red's shoulders. And if he let Ret die, Luke McQuade would kill him.

Milly stood at the head of the bed. She was the only girl whose concern for the wounded man was real. She bent over him to brush a damp cloth over his brow. Ret's eyes opened, and he raised his hand to push her away from him. His gaze locked on Red's face.

"Where's Luke?" His voice was weak.

Red said, "He should be riding in any time."

Ret's face was pinched with pain as he sucked in a deep breath. "Get me that Grover girl," he said harshly. He pushed himself up on one elbow. "I don't want any floozy taking care of me."

Milly's face whitened. She tossed the damp face-cloth at Ret, whirled, and left the room. The other girls snickered, but slowly backed off as Ret turned to look at them.

"Get her!" Ret ordered.

Red hesitated; then his glance went to Slim, who was standing at the foot of the bed. He nodded. "All right; I'll get her." He made a motion to Slim, and they both left the room.

Ret Blue coughed, and a thin streak of blood stained the corner of his mouth. He wiped it with the back of his hand, his eyes pained, then sank back slowly on the bed, his gaze seeking out one of the men who had remained.

"Get me a bottle," he whispered. "I want to be around when Luke comes." A long moment passed as his eyes closed; then his mouth tightened harshly. "Got something to tell Luke."

PAUL GROVER was just coming out of the luggage room when Red and Slim came into the station. He hesitated a split-second too long before turning for the rifle he had propped up in a corner.

Red intercepted him, shoved him hard against the wall, then picked up the rifle, stepped back, and half turned to face Betty, who had swung around on her stool at the ledger table.

Red said thinly, "Just sit tight, ma'am, and you won't get hurt." He looked back to Paul, who was eying him, afraid yet desperate. "You, too, Mr. Grover. Nobody gets hurt unless you get foolish."

Paul said bitterly, "What do you want?"

Red nodded to Slim, who came up to him. He handed the lanky long-rider Paul's rifle.

"I've come for your daughter."

Paul started to come at Red, but Slim jammed the rifle muzzle against his stomach and cocked the hammer.

Betty's eyes dilated. She screamed, "No, no, Father!"

Red turned to her. "You come quietly, and no one'll get hurt," he repeated coldly.

Betty shrank back against the table. "Go where?"

"The Pecos Bar, ma'am," Red said. He didn't like this, and some of it showed in his face. "Ret Blue's been shot. He needs someone to look after him."

Paul said harshly, "Why my daughter? She's no doctor!"

Red shrugged. "She'll do, I reckon, until Doc Blake gets back." He turned to Betty. "It wasn't my idea. Ret asked for you."

Betty stared at him, fear in her eyes. "No," she said tautly. "I can't help him."

Red eyed her for a moment. "I'm sorry, ma'am, but Ret asked me to fetch you." He glanced at Paul. "Luke McQuade will be in town before dark. You know how he feels about his brother." He turned back to Betty. "I don't care if you can help him or not, but I'm taking you to the Pecos Bar."

Betty nodded resignedly, sensing the cold determination in the man. She looked at her father. "I'll be all right," she said. "Doctor Blake should be back soon." She swung around to join Red. "I won't be needed then, will I?"

Red shrugged. "I shouldn't think so, ma'am." He looked at Slim. "Stay here with Mr. Grover—" his smile held little humor—"just to remind him he's got work to do."

He waited as Betty put on her coat and took an umbrella. He followed her outside into the thin, slanting rain.

Slim checked Paul's rifle casually, ejected the shells and shoved them into his pocket. He set the rifle up against the wall and slid his palm down over his holstered Colt in a silent warning to Paul Grover, but Paul wasn't watching him. Grover was staring at the door, a stricken, bitter look in his eyes.

In the office, the telegraph receiver began to click, its metallic sound insistent against the stillness. Paul turned then, roused by the repeated clicks. He sat down stiffly before the key and started to take down the incoming message.

THE GRAY DAY worsened. Matt Vickers had brought out his slicker, but the driving rain man-anaged to get through it, chilling him. He had followed the iron rails west out of Fulton. Paul's directions had been explicit, but at that he almost missed the gully under the railroad bridge.

He paused there to get his bearings. He had the sudden prickly feeling that he was being followed, but, looking back, he saw no one. He was usually ruled by instinct in these matters, and ordinarily he would have circled and checked on his back trail. But the day was miserable and visibility poor; he decided he was getting a little jumpy and put his uneasiness behind him.

Matt followed the gully, running a foot deep in water off the low hills ahead. When he came to the point where the gully angled between narrow rock shoulders, he knew he was close to his destination.

He still couldn't make out the shack. He let his horse drift against the rain and wiped his face with his neckerchief. Curiously, his thoughts were with Doc Emory—he kept seeing the strain in the ex-Ranger's face. Doc had never gotten

over having been forced to resign from the
Ranger force. Accepting the town marshal's job
today had been a gesture which underlined Doc's
bitter regret.

Vickers' horse sloshed through fetlock-deep
water and rounded a massive rock jutting like a
prow ahead of them. Suddenly the cabin lay
ahead of Matt, small and sagging in the gray
afternoon light. An open-sided lean-to housed a
mule and a scrubby bronc. Someone had thought
enough of their comfort to string a blanket across
the open to protect the animals from the rain. The
mule eyed Vickers with a sad-eyed stare; the
bronc showed yellow teeth in a welcoming snicker.

Matt reined in before the closed cabin door.
He remained in the saddle, sensing that he was
being watched through a crack in the flimsy door
panels. He was not mistaken. The door scraped
open, and Joe Ivers filled the opening. He was
holding a shotgun in his hands.

"It's a terrible day," Matt observed pleasantly.

"It shore is," Joe agreed. But he remained
otherwise inhospitable, his eyes narrowed, suspicious. "A terrible day for visiting."

Foley showed up behind his partner now, unshaven, unkempt. His bleary eyes added their
hostility to that of Joe Ivers.

Matt asked, "Mind if I come inside?"

"Why?"

It was a fair question, under the circumstances, and Matt decided there was no longer need to conceal his identity. He reached inside his coat pocket, brought out his identification and badge and held it out for Joe and Foley to see.

"A United States marshal," Joe muttered, surprised, and a new look of cautious respect appeared in his eyes.

Matt put his gaze on Foley. "I came out to ask you about that angel you saw, the one riding a white horse."

The two men stared at him. Joe Ivers cursed, but it was an automatic reflex, without rancor.

He said, "Foley, I told you you talk too much."

He made a motion with the shotgun. "Step down, Marshal. Reckon we can rustle up a cup of coffee for you."

Matt dismounted. He looped his reins around the pommel, thereby giving his horse freedom of movement. The horse immediately moved away from the driving rain, tossing his sleek head in dislike, and sought the scant shelter of the cabin's lee wall.

Matt followed Joe into the cabin. It had a wooden floor, which surprised him. The boards

were scuffed and old, and the cracks between
them were wide enough to throw debris into.
There was a fire going in the small rickety cast-
iron range set close to the rear wall. A rusted
pipe went straight up through the roof. Rain
seeped through to make dark stains on the pipe.

A hand lantern was set on a homemade table
in the middle of the room. Two bunks and a couple of packing cases completed the furnishings.

There was but one window, in the left wall,
which let in a gray light. Matt blinked to get ac-
customed to the gloom.

Foley was mumbling, "United States marshal
—out here?" He turned to Vickers. "You knew
Sheriff Billens?"

Matt nodded. "I'm Matt Vickers."

Joe said, "I've heard Tom talk about you."
He laid his gun aside and held out his hand.
"Darned glad to meet you, Marshal."

Matt took Joe's hand. Behind them Foley was
fumbling around in a wooden box. He found a
battered tin cup which he gave a cursory wiping
before pouring coffee into it from the pot on the
stove. The coffee was as black as sin and smelled
faintly like burnt dog's hair.

"Glad you dropped by, Marshal," Joe said.
"I was getting tired of listening to Foley's danged

sea stories." He grinned sourly. "Foley's like an old woman when he gets to gabbing, and worse when he's getting over a whizzdinger like last night's celebration."

Matt grinned. "Gets bad enough to start seeing angels on white horses?"

"Well, I wasn't drunk when I saw her," Foley protested. "I was coming back from the Conchos, north of here. Went alone this time. Joe had a spell of rheumatism and stayed behind. Panned some dust—enough to keep us in grub for a couple more months—and felt pretty good. I come back by way of Red Canyon, an' Mabel, my mule, kept wanting to go east. Couldn't argue with her nohow—she's got a mind like a danged mule when she gets that way—so I give her her head. We came down by the Indian Tanks country, and right then I decided to take a look at the old Spanish diggings."

Matt interrupted, "You mean there are old mines out there?"

Foley nodded. "Yup. Was quite a layout in the days when the Mexicans owned Texas. Sort of a little village still setting there. There's a big adobe house and three adobe barracks where the Injun workers lived. Mines petered out a long time ago, though, and the place has kind of gone to seed—"

Joe broke in, "Foley and me have been out there two or three times. Every once in a while we did a little work in one of the old shafts, hoping we'd hit it lucky and uncover a vein the old owners missed." He shrugged. "Never found anything, though."

Matt sipped some of the bitter brew in his cup. "The girl on the white horse?" He brought the subject back to Foley's wandering thoughts. "You sure you saw her?"

"Oh, yeah," Foley grunted. "Joe here didn't believe me. But I saw her, riding a white mare. She was rigged up in one of them fancy riding outfits, too. She stopped on the ridge just west of the Tanks. Mebbe she saw me, but she seemed just to be looking at the scenery. Then some blasted galoot put a slug through my hat."

He turned to find the abused headgear, and the first shot came through the window then, breaking the glass, smothering the thin jangle with its heavy report.

The slug knocked Matt Vickers back against the wall. He fell limply, not even touching his gun. His hat rolled from his head, and his face was smeared with blood.

Joe made an instinctive jump for the shotgun

and fell over it as the Colt outside the window blasted again.

Foley, caught off balance, remained stupefied for a moment too long. He had turned toward the window at the first shot, and he saw the killer's face as a blur behind the Colt. Foley lunged for the window, his hands curling. It was a blind, unreasoning move on his part. The Colt blasted almost in his face.

He stumbled back and fell against the rickety stove and overturned it. The lids popped off and rolled across the floor, and embers spilled out on the dry floor boards.

The cruel face in the shattered window eyed the limp figures. His attention centered on the lamp on the table. His Colt blasted once more. The lantern jumped off the table, a hole in its base, and smashed onto the floor. Kerosene dribbled out of it, soaking the boards. When it reached the nearest ember, there was a bluish white puff of flame that strengthened quickly as it raced along the kerosene path to the lantern.

The killer withdrew. Moments later the faint sound of his departure on horseback came back to the rain-swept clearing.

The fire within the cabin grew.

X

DOC EMORY stirred. There was a sharp pain in his head which made him close his eyes almost immediately. He lay quiet for a long moment, his thoughts jumbled and hazy. A sound was trying to intrude on his awareness, but it was some moments before he brought it into focus.

Someone was knocking on a door. He opened his eyes again, and now he saw that he was lying face up on a cot in one of the cells. The knocking seemed to come from a far distance. But it was determined, insistent; it pushed Doc up to a sitting position on the cot. He turned to face the door.

The movement sent blood pounding through his head, and for a moment he thought he'd be sick. He brought his hands up to his face and waited, forcing his will on his queasy stomach. After a moment the wave of nausea receded. He staggered to his feet and lurched to the cell door. He found it locked.

There was no one in the small office. The knocking on the outside door was impatient.

Doc croaked: "Come on in."

George Melvin came into the office. It was late in the afternoon, and a premature dusk had invaded the office. Melvin looked around, an impatient, faintly angry man. Then he turned and stared at Doc Emory in obvious surprise as Doc called out to him.

"I'm locked up in here. Get me out!"

Melvin stood like a man in a stupor. He said slowly, "I came to tell you that Luke McQuade and a couple of his riders just rode into town. They've crossed the bridge into New Town."

Doc Emory rattled the cell door. "Dammit, man, get me out of here!"

The newspaper publisher finally seemed to realize Doc's plight. He crossed to the cell door, tried it. Then he turned to the battered desk and searched through the drawers for the cell keys. He turned a puzzled look on the new town marshal.

"They're not here," he muttered. He walked back to the cell. "What happened? How'd you get locked up in there?"

Doc's fingers tightened around the cell bars. "It's a long story," he said bitterly. His lips tightened. "What time is it?"

George Melvin plucked a gold watch from his

vest pocket. "A few minutes after four."

A sickness deeper than his pain showed briefly in Doc Emory's eyes. He had been out almost five hours. Concussion. His fingers reached up to probe gently at the tender swelling behind his left ear. It was lucky the blow hadn't killed him.

Melvin spotted the streak of dried blood down the side of Doc's face and reacted to it. "You're hurt, man. You need medical attention." He started to turn away. "I'll get Doctor Blake."

"Get someone who can break me out of here!" Doc interrupted harshly.

Melvin looked back at Emory, pity in his eyes. He nodded. "I'll get Jake," he said quietly. "He's the blacksmith."

He turned and went outside, and in the stillness Doc could hear the ticking of the wall clock above the desk. He turned and walked back to the cot, sat down and put his aching head between his hands.

A small bitter voice was whispering in his head, taunting him. He had trusted the kid, blinded himself to the man's lies because he had needed him.

God help me, Doc thought bitterly, *I needed him!*

He was remembering Kip's smooth, disarming

talk, then the cold-eyed youngster's quick chopping blow.

Kip was gone, and Emory knew that once again he had failed his badge. He had put a killer at Marshal Vickers' elbow, under the guise of a friend, and now he felt a terrible futility as he sat there in the semi-gloom, a small, bitterly disheartened man.

He had waited ten years for a chance to redeem himself, with the law *and his own son.*

He stood up and walked slowly to the door, waiting for George Melvin to return. The thin drizzle outside misted the dirty window; it was no more dismal than the small man's inner torment.

He stood looking out into the small, dingy office a thousand miles from where he was born—a place he hardly knew. He was looking back down the bitter years, trying to find out where he had failed, how he had failed. For he *had* failed a lot of people.

Once it had been a woman who had borne him a son—a woman he had not married. The boy had grown up to hate him. How deeply that hate had been instilled in his son by his mother Doc Emory only now realized. He had tried to go back to her years later. He had found her in a border

town, living with another man, and she had
laughed at him and cursed him. He had gotten
drunk and gone looking for the man who lived
with her and killed him. He hadn't known until
years later than the man was Frank Evers, that
his son had looked upon Frank Evers as his
father.

Doc had not seen Lou again until he had reached
Paseo a few days ago. Lou's mother was dead.
But the boy remembered Emory. Only he was no
longer a boy; he was a man Doc Emory didn't
know—a killer whose gun was for hire, whose
code was treachery.

Doc had thought he could make up to his son
for the years he had ignored him, but he knew
now that Lou had come to him in Paseo only to
use him; had met him in that small border town
only because Lou knew that Doc Emory was a
friend of Matt Vickers and because Lou had
somehow known that Marshal Vickers was headed
for Fulton.

Doc's hands gripped tightly around the cell
bars again. Whatever Lou was up to, Doc had to
stop him. *He had to*! He owed that much to Matt
Vickers—to himself.

GEORGE MELVIN returned five minutes later

with Jake, a brawny man carrying a pinch bar.
It took the blacksmith less than two minutes to
snap the worn lock and get Doc out of the cell.

Doc Emory crossed to the scarred desk and
rummaged around for his Colt. He wasn't surprised to find that his gun was not there. He
turned to Melvin and the blacksmith, who were
staring expectantly at him.

"I need a gun in good working order," he said
grimly.

"I've got a pistol in my office, a thirty-two,"
the newspaper publisher offered.

Doc shook his head. "I'm used to something
heavier." He glanced outside. "Maybe I can pick
one up at the hardware store."

Jake interrupted. "I've got Sheriff Billens'
Colt at my place."

Doc crossed to him. "Let's go get it."

Melvin said sharply, "Wait a minute, Emory!"
As Doc turned to face him, frowning: "You
going after Luke McQuade alone?"

Doc eyed him for a moment, a small man de-
ciding his fate. He could not wait until Vickers
returned from whatever errand he had gone on.
This, he reflected bitterly, was his own problem.
He had made it; now he would have to take
care of it.

"No," he replied quietly to the newspaper man, "not Luke. Someone else first."

He went out into the thin drive of rain with Jake. Melvin waited inside the office for a moment, staring into the muddy street. He felt uneasy and faintly resentful at the way events had shaped themselves. Last night things had seemed simpler.

Now, as he felt the wet chill of the dying day seep into him, he began to feel afraid. He had talked the town commissioners into hiring as town marshal a man whom they knew little about; the man they had chosen to wear Sheriff Tom Billens' badge had turned out to be only a small, pathetic man.

George went out finally, closing the office door behind him. He didn't follow Doc and the blacksmith. Instead, he cut back to his own office. He stepped inside, a mounting trepidation tightening his lips.

A tall, gangly sixteen-year-old boy was setting type in a case. Melvin walked up, picked up the copy from which the boy was setting type, crumpled it in his fist and dropped it into the wastebasket.

"Go on home, Pete," he told the boy. "I'll call you in the morning—" his lips twisted wryly—

"if we're still in business."

He watched the boy put on his coat and go out into the slackening rain. He stood by the window for a long moment, then turned to his desk and pulled open a drawer.

A small, silver-plated pistol stared up at him. Melvin was not without experience with a hand gun. No frontier editor lived long without encountering violence of one kind or another—from irate readers or drunken politicians who had felt the sting of his editorial dislike.

But Luke McQuade was of another breed. This was not an angry reader; this was a cold, professional gunman. And he would not be coming after Melvin with a horsewhip or a shotgun.

Melvin sighed. He was facing again the choices he had confronted in other towns. He could pack what he could and drift again, to set up shop in another place, another town.

Or he could stay.

He sagged tiredly into his chair, stared bleakly toward the window. He was tired of moving on. He would live or he would die in Fulton.

His fingers tightened around the silver-plated pistol as he waited.

XI

LUKE McQUADE hunched over his saddle, his slicker flapping across his thick shoulders. A trickle of cold rain worked its way down between his shoulder blades. He suffered it without comment, taking it as he took most things that happened to him, quietly and without complaining.

He was a raw-boned man, six feet of bone and gristle and taut muscle; a hard and merciless man. He had been born on a small, hard-rock farm in Ohio, and he had been fourteen before he had eaten enough to fill his gaunt belly. His father had died when he was two, and his mother had remarried a cheap tinhorn with a smooth tongue and a bad back. Luke remembered only that his stepfather drank a lot, talked a lot, but seldom worked. A few years after Ret was born, the man drifted off.

His mother supported the two boys until she died of overwork and passed the burden of Ret on to Luke. And in a perverse way Luke had kept looking after Ret, although he was thirty now, and Ret only two years younger. He never gave it much thought; his mother had asked him to look after Ret, and he did. He didn't question it. But maybe at the core of this flinty-eyed killer was the need to hold onto something, a point of reference in an otherwise hard and bitterly un- rewarding life.

He rode now with two men at his side. Luke had completed his job at Track Town and was on his way back when Lafe intercepted him with the news that his half-brother had been shot. Lafe was the dark, quiet man at his right; Bibs Jen- kins, chunky and usually talkative, rode at his left stirrup. Like Lafe, he was quiet tonight.

They turned instinctively toward the Gay Dog Saloon, their usual rendezvous in Fulton. But Red Slater hailed them as they came by the Pecos Bar.

"Luke!"

Luke turned and rode up to the walk where Red waited under the protection of the wooden awning. Red said quietly, "He's still alive, Luke.

In here."

Luke dismounted, the other two following suit. He followed Red inside the dimly lighted, quiet bar where a few of his men lounged at the counter, waiting for him. Surprise made a small V between Luke's eyes, but he kept his silence, knowing explanations would come later.

He went upstairs, and Red opened the door to Vicki Barnes' quarters and stepped aside to let Luke through.

The first thing Luke saw was Betty Grover standing at the head of the big, flower-covered bed. Ret had his right hand clasped about hers; his eyes were closed, but his chest rose and fell in uneven breathing.

One of Luke's men was on guard inside, lounging in a chair against the far wall.

Luke stared with a gunmetal, expressionless gaze at Betty Grover. Her face was flushed, defiant, as she stared back at him. Curtly then Luke made a motion to the guard; the man got to his feet and went outside, closing the door behind him. Red had followed Luke into the room. He waited by the door as Luke walked slowly to his brother and looked down at him.

Ret sensed his approach. He said weakly,

"Red?" His eyes remained closed.

Luke said, "It's me, Ret. Luke."

Ret's eyes flicked open. His gaze focused slowly on Luke's face. A twitch of a smile touched his lips.

Luke asked: "How are you?"

"Not good," Ret answered.

Betty Grover started to pull away, but Ret's fingers tightened on hers, holding her.

"Stay," he whispered to her. "Makes me feel better."

Luke cut in, his voice even, hiding the emotion inside him. He was always cold, this man, even with the women he frequented—cold and hard.

"Who shot you?"

Ret's eyes shifted to him. "Matt Vickers."

Luke started, a small shock of surprise showing briefly in his gaze.

"Vickers? The United States marshal?" Then, hard: "You sure, Ret?"

Ret tried to nod, but found it too much effort. He said, "Yes," instead. "Had to stay alive to tell you."

He was silent for a long moment, regrouping his fading forces. On the other side of the bed

Betty Grover was thinking of the tall quiet man who had come into her life, the man she had known only as Matt.

She pulled away from Ret's loosening grip, and as she stepped back Ret rolled his head toward her, his lips twisting in pain.

"Never wanted to hurt you," he said to Betty. "Only wanted to be—" His voice faded, and his eyes closed as if he were suddenly very tired.

Luke looked at her, his eyes bleak. Of Red, standing by the door, he asked: "What's she doing here?"

Red came up to the foot of the bed, glancing at Betty. "Ret wanted her here," he said. "Doc Blake was out of town. Ret didn't want anyone else to take care of him."

Luke frowned. "Rode by the Doc on the way in. He was stranded about four miles out of town; buggy wheel busted." A thin smile touched his lips. "Offered him a ride back, but he said hell'd freeze over before he took anything from the likes of me."

His smile was humorless but without rancor. He looked at Betty. "Stay with him," he ordered. And then, his eyes holding hers, going grim as he sensed her resentment, "He better be alive when I come back!"

He motioned to Red; they walked to the door and went out. The gun guard returned inside, closing the door behind him.

In the hallway Red said worriedly, "He's got a fifty-fifty chance." And then, tightly, "No chance at all, though, if that bullet doesn't come out of him."

Luke nodded. "I'll send Lafe back for Doc Blake." They started down the stairs to the badly lighted barroom, where Lafe and Bibs had joined the others at the bar. They were drinking in morose silence. The swamper who had gone out for Red right after Ret had been shot lay slumped in a drunken stupor over a corner table, his hand still clutching an empty bottle.

Luke surveyed the scene for a moment. Then, "Why here?" he asked coldly. "Where's the woman who runs this place, Vicki Barnes?"

"She's dead," Red answered. "That's what started it all, I guess," he added slowly. He shook his head. "Ret can't be right, Luke, not about the man who shot him."

Luke looked at him, frowning.

"Matt Vickers," Luke cut in coldly. "Has to be. I was told he was coming." He turned and looked back up the stairs. "Ret just happened to run into him before I got back." His lips pulled back almost wolfishly against his teeth. "Vickers was to be my man, Red."

Red shrugged. "Why would he want to kill Mrs. Barnes?"

Luke's gaze tore into him. "Killed who?"

"Raney and your brother followed Vickers in here," Red explained. "They saw him go up the outside stairs, crawl in through the bedroom window. Raney followed him through the window, and Vickers killed him. Ret had come inside here and was waiting for Vickers to come down those stairs. Vickers shot him." Red made a small gesture. "I wasn't here, but Ret told us that much. We brought Ret up to the bedroom, and it was then we saw the woman. She was sprawled out on her couch—dead."

"Shot?"

Red frowned. "That's the funny part of it," he admitted. "Just dead. Not a mark on her."

Luke crossed to the bar beside Lafe, and as the dark gunslinger turned to look at him, he said: "Take another drink; then ride back and pick up Doc Blake. Haul him back any way you have to, long as he's alive when you get here!"

Lafe grimaced slightly at the unpleasant prospect of riding out into the rain again. But he finished his drink and went out.

Luke picked up a clean glass and poured himself a drink. Red waited until Luke downed his first shot of the burning rye whiskey before he added: "That ain't all that's happened since you've been away. We got ourselves a new town marshal, too; took the place of Sheriff Billens."

Luke slowly put his empty glass down on the counter, turned.

"Someone I know?"

Red nodded. "Doc Emory."

Luke's dark face remained impassive. "Matt Vickers and Doc Emory," he murmured, and poured himself another drink. Then, low, grimly: "Where are they?"

"Emory was in the law office, last I knew. Matt rode out of town." Red shrugged. "I thought he was just another gunman who found out what he had gotten himself into and was hightailing it." He frowned. "I guess maybe he was riding out to Track Town to find you."

Luke shook his head. "Didn't see him."

He finished his second drink, shoved the glass aside. "Who hired Doc?"

"That newspaperman, George Melvin. Him and that town commissioner, John Carlson. Formed a citizens' committee to bring law and order back to Fulton."

Luke nodded absently. "I'll take care of them later." His palm slid down over the cold holster pouching his gun. "We'll take care of Doc Emory first."

He turned to the door, and Red followed him.

THE GAY DOG was a block south of the Pecos Bar. It was an illy-lighted, raffish bar that served rotten liquor, dice, cards and a long back room lined with scarred and dirty bunks for those who, unable to make it to other quarters, slept off the remaining hours of the night.

It was a place of easy entry and exit, with the low hills riding just a few hundred yards behind it. It was admirably suited to most of the Gay Dog's customers who, as a rule, were men who lingered a day or two and then moved on.

It was one of the first places Sheriff Billens had closed during his short term as law officer in Fulton. It was reopened and taken over by the McQuade bunch shortly after they came to town.

It was a jerry-built, sagging structure at best,

and now the unpainted, rain-streaked boards gave it an even more dismal aspect. This was where Lou Evers, alias Kip Billens, waited.

Kip was a one-drink man. He sipped it slowly, one eye on the clock, and when it indicated four-thirty, he pushed his glass away and walked outside.

He saw Luke ride into town, clattering across the plank bridge with two of his riders, watched him get called to the Pecos Bar by Red. Kip was only mildly interested. Luke's job was done here, but the longrider didn't know it yet.

He started to build himself a cigarette. The misting rain held a chill. He finished licking it into shape, stuck it into his mouth and was reaching for a match when he saw Doc Emory.

The man was coming across the bridge, alone— a small, tired-looking man with a gun showing plainly on his hip. A small frown settled between Kip's eyes; he started to move back toward the Gay Dog, then thought better of it.

He waited on the corner, just under the protecting awning. Slowly he took the cigarette from his mouth, tucked it carefully into his shirt pocket; then his right hand slid down, and his thumb hooked just above his holstered gun.

Doc Emory was his father, but Kip had never thought of the man in that way, and no loyalty stirred in him now.

Doc Emory crossed the bridge and came walking toward him. He spotted Kip, and his step quickened a bit, and his gaze darkened with bitter questioning.

He was across the street from the Pecos Bar, going by, when Luke stepped out of the saloon. Red was with the longrider, but Luke waved him back when he saw Emory.

"Doc!" Luke called out.

Doc paused. Luke's voice was like a spear, pinning him; he was to be given no reprieve.

Up the street, on the corner, Doc's son waited, his thumb hooked in his cartridge belt.

Slowly Doc turned.

Luke stepped out into the muddy street, facing Emory. "You looking for me, Doc?" the killer asked.

The ex-Ranger eyed him with a faint impatience. The wind was picking up, and there was a raw chill to it. He said bitterly, "Not now, Luke," and started to turn away.

"No sense in waiting!" Luke snapped.

He was moving across the street, a dark, raw-boned, pushing man. "You come for me now, Doc, or—" he paused briefly as Doc stiffened— "you ride out of town!"

The tight knot of fear dissipated in the old man, and an inner voice mocked him. He thought with wry bitterness that the doctor who had told him he would die in bed of a bad heart was wrong.

He glanced at Kip. The youngster was still watching for him on the corner. This boy had told Matt that he was riding into Fulton to side with Doc and Matt—had told Vickers that he was Sheriff Billens' brother. Both had been lies. And yet it was not too late for Kip to make amends. He was fast with a gun. If he drew on Luke, between them they could—

Luke's voice slashed across his thoughts, bleak and prodding. "Well, now, Doc?"

Emory shrugged. He dropped his right hand to brush back the skirt of his long coat and drew, all in the same motion. He had only a glimpse of Luke moving. Then Luke's first shot ripped into his chest. He was falling back when the outlaw's second shot whirled him around; he tried to stay on his feet, tried to get his nerveless fingers to lift his gun from his holster. He didn't feel the last slug smash through the back of his head.

McQuade walked up to Doc's body, sprawled face down in the mud. He turned Emory over with his toe. Doc's badge caught the fading daylight, glinted. Luke bent over him, ripped it off and flung the metal symbol of authority down the street. His bright, deadly glance challenged the few onlookers peering from the shelter of doorways.

Then, without hurrying, Luke turned and went back into the Pecos Bar.

From the corner Lou Evers, alias Kip Billens, surveyed his father's body. There was no sign of emotion in his face. Slowly he reached inside his shirt pocket for his cigarette and put it between his lips. The match flare was reflected briefly in his eyes as he lighted up; then he turned away.

The fine rain sifted slowly over Doc Emory's body.

– XII –

GROUND-REINED on the lee side of the miners' cabin, Vickers' big stallion had heard the shots smash through the window on the other side. Gunwise, he had faded away into the rain-swept timber edging the small clearing. Now he circled a clump of aspens and stopped, looking back. The rain dripped steadily from the overhead branches.

He saw a lean figure detach itself from the side of the cabin and run toward a huge, gray-wet rock —the figure appeared a moment later, mounted on a bay horse, and faded quickly from sight.

The stallion waited for Matt to appear.

After a while he whinnied impatiently. He headed back for the cabin, his ears pricked alertly.

Tendrils of smoke were coming from the back of the shack. The big stallion circled around to the door. He whistled sharply for the federal officer.

Vickers did not come out. The stallion pawed the muddy ground. He walked to the door, nudged it. It gave slightly. He lifted his right forefoot and pushed against it, and the door creaked open and smoke snaked out, losing itself in the slanting rain.

Inside the cabin, the entire rear wall was in flames. The stallion shook his head. He nudged the door wide open and saw Vickers on the floor. His whicker was sharp, questioning.

Vickers did not stir.

The big stud's nostrils twitched as smoke bit sharply at them. He forced his bulk inside the shack, nickering impatiently.

There were two other men lying on the floor. The clothes of the short one were on fire, and there was an unpleasant smell in the smoke-filled room. But the horse was interested only in Vickers.

He closed his teeth on Matt's slicker-clad shoulder and jerked, hoping to rouse his master from the strange sleep he was in. Matt did not stir.

Alarm quivered through the big stallion. The smoke was beginning to hurt his eyes; the fire frightened him and caused a nameless dread. He snorted heavily, then took hold of Matt's shoulder with his teeth again and started to back away, dragging the U.S. marshal across the floor.

His rump came in contact with the door frame. He tried to force his way back through the entrance, but his maneuvering closed the door instead, trapping him.

Suddenly panicky, the stallion lashed out at the obstruction with powerful, iron-shod hind feet. The flimsy door splintered. He kept hammering away until he had kicked out almost the entire front of the shack.

He backed through the opening now, dragging Vickers with him. He kept backing up until he was well clear of the burning building. Then he stopped, lifted his head and sniffed the wind.

The rain was driving across the clearing, lashing the shack, fighting the stubborn flames. The stallion looked down at the man with whom he had ridden a thousand trails. A puzzled whinny vibrated in his throat. He nudged the limp figure again, hoping to awaken him.

It was a long time afterward when Vickers finally stirred. The big horse was standing over him like a dark, sleek statue, waiting.

Matt rolled over and came to his feet and pawed at the right holster. It was as though he were completing a motion barely begun when the ambusher's bullet had smashed across his skull, just over his right temple.

He staggered and fell against the stallion and reached out with blind instinct for the saddle pommel. He held on, his knees buckling, holding himself up with a blind effort of will and the quivering strength in his arms.

The stallion waited patiently.

Slowly the federal officer fought back the blackness that clouded his eyes. The all-engulfing pain in his head receded to a sharp ache, the turmoil in his stomach settled, and he took a deep, shaky breath.

He was muddy from having been dragged across the clearing, and thoroughly soaked from the rain. A chill went through him, and he shivered uncomfortably. He forced his eyes open, but there was a red mist in front of one, and the other was blurred.

Still holding onto the saddle horn with one hand, he reached in his pocket for a handkerchief. He wiped his face, his eyes, and saw rain-thinned blood darken the cloth. He reached up and touched the ugly wound over his temple.

Close, he thought emptily. *Closer to death than I've ever been.*

He pushed away from the stallion then, and found he could stand on his own. But there was a weakness in his knees, and his muscles quivered.

He stared at the cabin. The roof had caved in, and a side wall was still burning slowly, although the rain had all but put out the fire.

He walked unsteadily to the splintered doorway and, studying it, came to the realization of how he had gotten out. He could see Joe's body, with a section of the roof across him. Foley was a blackened lump, his clothes still smoking. An odor of scorched flesh came to Vickers. His stomach heaved, and he turned away, leaning weakly against the stallion's saddle.

There was nothing he could do for Foley and Joe. He was in no condition even to bury them.

But he would see to it, he promised himself grimly, that their killer would pay for this.

He ran his palm gently over his mount's neck. "Dragged me out, eh, boy?"

Slowly Matt pulled himself into the saddle. He felt the effort start blood pumping from the cut above his temple, felt it seep down his beard-stubbled cheek. He settled himself in the saddle; then, tight-lipped, he fashioned a bandage with his handkerchief, knotting it hard around his head.

He felt a slight dizziness come over him, and he gripped at the saddle horn to keep himself from sliding out of the saddle. In his present condition, he reflected grimly, he would be fair game for the killers in Fulton. But it was getting dark, and with luck he might ride into town unnoticed.

He turned the stallion away from the shack and rode in the general direction of Fulton.

— XIII —

IT WAS DARK when Lafe rode across the bridge into Fulton's new section and pulled up in front of the Pecos Bar. Doctor Blake was riding in front of him; in the lamplight reflecting up from the muddy puddles, Blake's face was grim, rebellious. He was holding his medical bag in front of him.

Lafe slid out of the saddle, reached up for the young railroad doctor and pulled him down beside the tired horse. Blake was thoroughly soaked. He glanced at the Pecos Bar, then turned to Lafe.

"I don't care about the Hippocratic oath!" he said bitterly. "I'm not tending a killer like—"

Lafe jabbed him against the side with the muzzle of his gun. His voice was soft, but iron firm.

"Tell Luke that, Doc. Tell him."

He motioned toward the door, and for a moment longer Blake balked; then, as Lafe palmed his gun and started to raise it, he nodded curtly and turned to the door.

Luke, morose, silent, was waiting at the bar with Red and Bibs. He came around as Lafe and Doctor Blake came inside and crossed quickly to meet them.

"He's upstairs, Doc," Luke said coldly. "He looks bad."

Roger Blake eyed the big outlaw. He was not without courage, but at this moment he was guided more by a combination of fear and anger than by common sense.

"There's nothing I can do for him," he said coldly. He started to turn away, but Luke grabbed him by the coat collar and jerked him around. The outlaw's eyes smoldered.

"You haven't looked at my brother yet!" he said bleakly. "How do you know?"

Blake stared at the man, a helpless bitterness shaping his words.

"I don't know—and I don't care."

He reeled back as Luke backhanded him across the mouth. He dropped to his knees, shaking his head; over him Lafe leveled his gun.

Luke pushed the man away. He bent over

Blake and jerked him to his feet.

"You'll care, Doc!" He jerked a thumb toward the stairs. "There's a girl up there with him. I think you know her—that station agent's daughter."

"*Betty*!" The name tore from Blake's lips.

"If my brother dies, she dies!" Luke said savagely. "Now, you going to look at him, Doc?"

Blake's eyes ranged over the men coming up beside Luke; he wiped the tiny streak of blood from his cut lips and nodded.

Luke picked up the medical bag Blake had dropped and shoved it into his hands. "The railroad must have thought you were pretty good," he said grimly. "Let's see how good you really are at your job, Doc!"

INSIDE THE BEDROOM, Betty moistened Ret's brow and watched his labored breathing with mixed feelings. Ret's eyes were closed, but he responded to her touch by reaching up and closing his fingers around her wrist. They had little strength in them.

He whispered, "Ma, I don't feel good," and Betty's hand froze, and terror came into her eyes. She glanced quickly at the gun guard seated by the door; the man was examining a dog-eared *Police Gazette* one of the saloon entertainers had given him.

She gently freed her hand, and Ret's arm fell limply across his chest. His eyes opened now, and he saw her.

He said, "Betty—" as if he wanted to tell her many things. But the name faded on his lips, and he sighed gently, closed his eyes, and his breathing stopped.

Slowly, numbly, Betty Grover straightened. She had hated this man's attentions, hated his rough, bumbling ways, hated him because he was Luke McQuade's brother. Yet she felt pity for him now; he had never meant to be anything other than gentle with her.

But would Luke understand? Would he?

She heard steps coming toward the door, and her thoughts congealed. She pressed back against the wall by the bed, her eyes glued on the door. The gun guard stood up as Luke came inside with Doctor Blake. Lafe, Red and Bibs remained in the doorway.

Doctor Blake's gaze went to Betty, and he misunderstood her terror. He crossed to her quickly, took her by the hand.

"Betty," he said, "it's all right now. I'll take care of him."

Slowly, wordlessly, Betty shook her head.

"It's all right!" Blake said sharply. He turned to Luke. "Let her go! I'll do what I can for Ret."

Luke nodded.

Blake pushed her gently toward the door. "Go on home, Betty. I'll join you later."

She shook her head. Her eyes were on Luke, her voice small, frightened. "Roger, he's dead."

Blake stared at her for a split-second, then whirled to the bed. Luke strode up beside him, bending over his brother. He watched Blake put the back of his palm against Ret's slightly open mouth; then Blake thumbed back Ret's eyelid.

Slowly then Blake straightened and looked at Luke.

Betty said tightly, "He died as you were coming up the stairs." Her eyes met Luke's as he turned to her. "There was nothing I could do."

Luke stood for a moment, staring at her. Then he looked back at his brother. Doctor Blake was examining the congealing froth of blood around the bullet hole in Ret's chest.

Roger said slowly, "Nothing I could have done for him, either." He turned to the girl, went to stand beside her; his arm went around her shoulder.

"No one could have saved him," he said to Luke. "But if you want to blame someone, blame me for not getting here earlier."

Luke eyed them. Whatever rage was flickering inside him, it showed only faintly in his eyes.

He said thickly, "Get out of here!"

Blake hesitated, eying the silent men by the door. Luke made a savage gesture with his hand. "I said to get out of here!"

Blake took Betty's hand. Together they left the room. Red Slater walked slowly to the bed and looked down at Ret's body. Luke had turned to the wall, hiding the spasm of inner torment. When he turned back, his face was dark, impassive again.

Red asked: "What are you going to do?"

Luke's eyes blazed with a cold, deadly light. "Find the man who killed him, Red—Matt Vickers!"

— XIV —

THE GUTTERING lamp in its wall holder
threw a yellow glare across Kip's inscrutable features as he stood beside Jake in Bryce Warner's
back room. He looked small beside the blacksmith, but the stogie stuck out of a corner of his
mouth at a jaunty angle, and he seemed only
slightly affected by the dead man lying on Warner's long embalming table.

Kip and Jake had brought Doc Emory's body
in a few minutes before.

Bryce, a small, nervous, white-haired man who
ran Fulton's only undertaking establishment,
was plainly not overjoyed at the sudden pickup in
business. He was standing by a closed coffin in a
corner of the room, his watery blue eyes ranging
from John Carlson and George Melvin, who stood
beside him, to Jake and Kip. His hands rubbed

nervously together as he muttered uneasily:

"I can't do anything until I get some sort of authorization." He looked at Kip. "I can't just bury anybody you bring in here."

Kip cut him off. "Couldn't leave him lying out there in the rain," he said coldly. "But if you don't want him in here—"

"He stays!" Carlson cut in sharply. The commissioner looked at the undertaker, frowning. "What's the matter with you, Bryce?"

"I don't want trouble," Bryce whined.

"He's dead," Carlson reminded him. "Dead men can't trouble anyone." He put his attention on Kip. "Can they, Mr. Billens?"

Kip shrugged. He reached inside his pocket, took out the badge he had found in the street and handed it to Carlson.

"I found it in the mud in front of the Pecos Bar," he said tonelessly. "I thought you might want it back."

Carlson's fingers tightened on the star. "I hoped you might want it, now that Doc Emory's dead."

"Me?" Kip's voice was amused.

"You're Tom Billens' brother, aren't you?"

Kip's eyes glittered briefly with a mocking

light. "That doesn't make me a fool like he was—or Doc."

Melvin reacted with a touch of bitter anger. "Your brother died trying to keep law and order here. Luke's men hanged him. Doesn't that mean anything to you?"

Kip shrugged. "I'll settle with Luke McQuade in my own way," he said softly.

Carlson thrust the badge into his pocket. He glanced at Doc's body. "How well did you know him?"

Kip spread his hands in a gesture indicating he had not know Doc too well. "I ran into him outside of town. He was riding this way, and I joined him." He frowned. "Doc said he had once been with the Rangers."

"That all you know about him?" Melvin snapped.

Kip turned his gaze on the irate newspaperman, studying him with a cold regard.

"Yes."

Melvin's voice indicated a harsh dislike of Kip. "Doc called you his partner this morning. He seemed to think you'd stand up with him against Luke."

"I can't help what Doc said," Kip intruded

bleakly. "He knew who I was. Maybe he was doing some wishful thinking. I advised him against taking the job."

"What about the tall stranger, the one who called himself Matt?" Carlson asked. "The man who shot up some of Luke's men in the Pecos Bar. Didn't you know him?"

Melvin added harshly, "You three were together in the bar last night."

"Just a coincidence," Kip replied. "Doc knew him, I guess. I didn't."

He rubbed his gloved right hand down his thigh, wiping some of Doc's blood from the skin-tight leather.

"Sorry I can't help you more, gentlemen," he said. He glanced at the battered alarm clock on a shelf behind the lamp; the lateness of the hour seemed to have meaning for him. He turned to leave.

"Do you know where that tall man went?" Carlson asked. "Maybe if he knew about Doc—"

Kip, at the door, shook his head. "I think he was headed for the Border. I know if I was him, that's where I would be headed."

"Why did you come to Fulton?" Melvin rasped.

"To visit my brother's grave," Kip said softly.

There was hidden laughter lurking behind his eyes. "Good night, gentlemen."

His glance shifted from them, to hold for one last brief moment on the still body of his father; then he went out.

It was quiet in the back room for a long moment after Kip left. Finally Carlson looked at the brooding newspaper publisher.

"*Pay me what you think I'm worth,*" he said, quoting Doc. He took a deep, bitter breath, sighed.

"The least we can do is bury him, George."

THE DAY had faded into darkness, and with the darkness even the drizzle stopped. A warmer wind came out of the south, sending vague tendrils toward the dark sky.

Far out on the plains to the east, a train whistled. The sound came to Paul Grover, waiting, taut and impatient, by his desk.

He shot a quick glance at Slim Favor lounging in a chair. Fred had come in, only to be sent home by McQuade's man. Fred was old, and there was no fight in him, no danger.

Paul Grover walked to the door and stared out across the wet platform toward town. Behind him,

Slim shifted his rifle to the crook of his arm and stood up, eying Paul silently, not without some sympathy. He knew what was bothering the station agent.

"She'll be all right," he said. "Luke doesn't make war on women."

Paul stared out into the night, unrelieved by the man's words. Fulton seemed quiet now, quieter than usual. He wondered with a dry mouth what Betty was going through.

The train sounded again, a warning note trembling high on the night.

Slim came up to stand behind him; he looked up the tracks. "Didn't know a train was due in this late."

His comment brought Paul's thoughts back to his work, and he remembered the telegram he had locked up in his safe—Marlowe's wire, advising him of the payroll's arrival.

Everything depended on secrecy. Not even the men on the train knew they were delivering the Desert Line's payroll.

Marlowe had trusted him to see that it went out to the laborers at Track Town.

Behind him the wire began clicking again, its dit, dit, dah sounding sharply and urgently. Slim turned, eying the clattering receiver for a moment.

"What's it say, Pop?"

Paul pushed past him into the office. He stopped by the desk, picked up a pencil and with his free hand tapped out an acknowledgement.

The message came through now. He started to write it down, stopped as he felt Slim looking down over his shoulder. Then, as the message stopped, he added a few words to the pad and pushed it aside.

"Who's Kip Billens?" Slim asked curiously, eying the words Paul had written down.

Paul shrugged. "Someone who claimed he was related to Sheriff Billens." He stood up now, feeling the pressure of time prod him.

"Look," he said bitterly, "I won't run away. And I'm not foolish enough to think I can help my daughter by going after her with a gun." He looked toward the door. "The train is due here in less than five minutes. If the boys in the cab see you here, there might be trouble."

Slim shrugged. He was tired of hanging around the station anyway. And he knew Grover was talking sense about not wanting to jeopardize his daughter.

By this time Luke should have arrived in town. He should be getting back to the Pecos Bar to see what was going on.

"Tell you what," he said to Grover. "I'm going down the street for a bite to eat. Bring you back some coffee?"

Grover nodded. "Be obliged to you."

He watched Slim walk to the edge of the platform, step down and turn the corner of the station. He thought he heard a muffled shot, but the train's whistle, loud now, blanketed it. He stared toward the corner, frowning, wondering if he *had* heard anything.

The engine's probing headlight cut the darkness along the tracks, splashing over the platform. Paul stepped up to meet it as it rumbled in, escape steam hissing in the night.

The fireman leaned out of the cab on Paul's side and waved to the station agent. Paul waved back mechanically.

The engine rolled past, its weight shaking the platform. Three cars were hooked up behind the tender, two coaches and the baggage car.

Paul stared at the empty coach windows, feeling tired and defeated.

The couplings clashed with iron harshness,

and a shudder went through the train. A conductor stepped off the last coach and waited on the platform. A few passengers stepped off, coming past Paul, heading for town.

The baggage door slid open, and two half-empty mail sacks were dumped onto the platform. Paul walked over to greet the messenger.

The man wore bib overalls. He peered into the darkness along the platform beyond Paul. Reassured, he turned to the safe inside the baggage car, opened it, and handed Grover a locked iron box.

The station agent took it without comment. The conductor was on the platform, waiting for him as he walked by. Up ahead, the engine panted like some tired monster catching its breath.

"No passengers?"

Paul shook his head. "No passengers." This had been a special run to Fulton. He saw the look on the conductor's face, and he knew what the man was thinking. A waste of money—how long could a railroad operate like this?

"Well, we'll be rolling," the man said. He walked back to the end coach, waving his lantern. He stepped inside as the engine lunged back against the cars, and as the train rolled past

Grover the fireman waved cheerfully once more.

Paul left the mail sacks lying on the platform and went inside the office with the iron box. He put the payroll on the desk by the safe; the message he had locked up inside bothered him. He read it once more, frowning, then put it inside his pocket.

He didn't hear the catlike footsteps on the platform behind him.

He picked up the box and started to put it inside the safe. In the morning, he thought, he'd take the handcar and roll it into Track Town and pay the men. It would keep the Desert Line alive a little longer.

How much longer?

But something else kept nagging at him. Frowning a little, he stood up, turned to the desk and found the small iron key with its cardboard tag. He turned back to the safe, knelt by the iron payroll box and unlocked it.

He didn't hear the man who paused briefly just inside the station, then started quickly for him. Paul Grover was staring down into the box, not believing what he saw.

Then he caught a glimpse of a muddy boot alongside him; he reacted to it too late. He was just starting to turn when the palmed Colt came down across his head. Paul Grover slumped forward with a sigh.

The intruder bent to pick up the payroll box. A look of surprise crossed his face. Then he clamped the lid down shut, locked it, and quickly left the station.

A heavy-set man was waiting for him in the darkness by the tool shed. He handed this man the payroll box.

The man chuckled. "Reckon this finishes the Desert Line, Lou, and all the suckers who backed it with their hard-earned money."

Lou, alias Kip, nodded. "I had to kill one of Luke's men. I didn't want to take the chance he'd come back while I was inside." His voice was colorless. "I rolled him under the platform."

"One less to worry about," the man said. Then, "You've done a good job, Lou. I'll see to it that you get a bonus."

"Thanks," Lou said dryly. He watched the man tuck the box under his arm. "Luke will be coming up to see you when he finds Vickers is dead. He'll be wanting his cut."

"Let him come," the man said. "I'll be ready for him. He'll get his cut, Lou—a six-ounce slug and an old mining shaft to hide his body." He chuckled again, pleased with the way things had gone. "I needed him in the beginning, him and his guns and his men. But not any more. I don't need anyone now."

"No one?" Lou's voice was soft.

"You, of course," the man said quickly. "I've needed you most of all."

Lou smiled thinly. "I'll stay in town tonight. I'll ride up with Luke in the morning, just to make sure we finish the job."

— XV —

SARAH, the Grover housekeeper, met Betty and Doctor Blake at the door. She was a stout woman in her early sixties who had been with the Grovers for more than five years; she had developed a motherly feeling toward Betty and a certain proprietary attitude toward Paul Grover.

"Well, now," she said rebukingly, "if you want supper, I'll have to reheat it."

"Supper can wait," Blake interrupted. "I think some good strong tea would be fine just now. Miss Grover has had a bad day."

They went inside, and the lamplight reflected from Betty's taut white face.

Sarah's attitude changed. "You poor girl," she said, leading Betty to the sofa. "You look all done in." Her glance came around to Blake. The young doctor looked somewhat disreputable in wet, muddy clothes, his upper lip beginning to puff.

Alarm quivered in Sarah's voice. "What happened, Doctor?"

"The tea," Blake reminded her firmly. "We could both use some."

"Of course, of course." Sarah nodded, flustered, turned and went into the kitchen.

Blake turned to Betty, who was lying back against the sofa pillows, her eyes half closed.

"The tea will do you good," he said. "I'd pass up supper tonight and go right to bed."

She shook her head. "I'm all right, Roger. No one hurt me." She breathed deeply. "It's Dad I'm worried about."

Roger said, "I'll see what I can do."

She clutched his arm. "Roger—" Her voice faltered. "They are violent men."

"I know," Blake replied. "But someone has to do something. The town can't die just because Luke McQuade is here."

"Someone has to," Betty agreed. "But not you, Roger." She saw a bitter look flash into his eyes and said quickly: "You don't have to prove yourself to me or to anyone. I saw you tonight—saw you face up to those men." Her eyes softened.

"Leave the shooting to someone else, Roger."

"Who?"

"That man, Matt. He's a United States marshal." She nodded at the doubting look in his eyes. "I heard Ret tell his brother before he died. His name is Matt Vickers."

Blake frowned. "Where is he?"

Betty shook her head. "He asked Dad for directions to some miner's shack somewhere out of town. I presume that's where he went. He promised he'd be back before night."

Blake studied her. "You think a lot of him, don't you?"

"Yes." Her hand tightened on his arm. "He's big and capable, and in times of violence like this he gives one a sense of security."

"I know," Blake conceded stiffly. "He's a better man than I am, isn't he?"

"In some ways," Betty said softly. Then, "Oh, Roger, don't you see?" Her eyes were turned up to him, shining with a deep tender light. "Matt is a good man, but he belongs to these violent times. He's needed now. But the future is built by men like you."

He looked at her, his stiffness melting at the warmth in her eyes. Slowly he bent over her.

"Roger," she whispered almost in his ear, "I don't want you to be hurt."

Her arms went around his neck as he kissed her.

Sarah came into the room with a tray. She paused as she saw them, a faint smile flickering around her mouth.

"Tea's ready," she said briskly.

Roger turned. Outside, a train whistle sounded, muted by the distance.

Betty sat up, turning toward the windows. "A train at this time of night?" She looked at Roger. "Must be a special run. I don't think Father knew."

Roger said, "I'll go see."

Sarah came up with the tray as Roger left. She set it down on the table in front of Betty.

"A nice young man," she said, and Betty nodded.

THE RAIN had stopped, but dark masses of high-moving clouds obscured the stars. Fulton's streets had a wet, deserted look; the lamplight spilling from behind steamy windows was ineffectual. What few people were about were dark, unseen shadows moving quickly to their destinations.

Doctor Blake paused by his office to listen to the train. It was moving away from the station; he could hear the heavy engine laboring more plainly now.

Whatever the reason for the unexpected run, it had been of short duration.

He unlocked the door to his office and walked through it to his bachelor quarters in the back. He changed swiftly, feeling better in dry clothes. He examined his cut lip in the mirror and knew he was lucky to have come away with so little physical damage.

He turned to the dresser, opened the top drawer, and looked at the pistol for a long moment before closing the drawer. Betty was right: he was not that good with a gun. For he felt a certain squeamishness about deliberately taking a human life.

He left the room, went out to the street and looked toward the railroad station a long quarter of a mile away. The train whistle floated back, already almost out of hearing.

About to start across the street, Blake paused, a shadow catching the corner of his eye. He turned and looked back down the dark, muddy street.

He thought he had seen a rider move out of an alley and cross toward Sheriff Billens' old office, a rider slumped over a saddle. But he saw no one now, and he wasn't sure. He waited a moment longer, a small worry nagging at him—that slumped figure had had a vague familiarity.

Blake shrugged. It could have been nothing more than a trick of his imagination.

He crossed the street and started toward the railroad station, his passage making a hollow sound on the wet plank walk. As he finally crossed to the small depot, mud muffled his approach. He came up the steps to the platform, and the first thing that caught his eye were the two mail bags still lying where the baggage man had dropped them.

Blake crossed slowly to the door, then stopped.

The old telegrapher, Fred, was kneeling beside Paul Grover, who lay in a crumpled heap in front of the open safe. Fred whirled as he heard Blake enter. Relief flooded his eyes as he saw who it was, but the fear did not entirely leave his seamed features.

"I just came in," he said. "Heard the train and wondered what brought it to Fulton. It wasn't on our regular schedule."

He watched Doctor Blake kneel beside Grover, examine him. "He was lying here." Fred held out a crumpled telegram. "This was on the ground beside him."

Blake took the telegram and read it.

"Payroll," Fred said. "Paul was the only one who knew."

Blake stared at the empty safe. What had happened was obvious. He felt despair envelop him. The Desert Line was through. It was implicit in Marlowe's telegram. It meant he was out of a job. But at the moment this mattered less than his concern for Paul Grover. He had to convince Betty and her father that the time had come to leave Fulton.

Fred said, "How bad is he hurt, Doctor?"

"I won't know until I get him home and make a better examination," Blake replied. "We'll need a carriage."

"Well, well," a hard voice interrupted, "you are a busy man tonight, aren't you, Doc?"

Blake turned. Fred shrank back from him, eying the men crowding into the small station.

Luke McQuade came up and glanced indifferently at Grover. "How is he?"

Blake's voice was tight. "Luckier than your brother was."

Luke eyed him for a moment, then glanced around the office. "Where's Slim?"

Blake shrugged.

Fred said, "Nobody was here when I came back. Just Mr. Grover."

Red Slater frowned. "I left him here to keep an eye on the girl's father."

Blake said slowly, "Looks like he did a bit more than that." As Luke studied him, eyes flinty, "The Desert Line payroll came in on that train that just left." He made a motion toward the open safe. "As you can see, there's no money in there now."

Luke's eyes flashed. He turned to Red Slater. "You know anything about the payroll arriving tonight?"

Red shook his head.

"Did Slim?"

"No." Red hesitated. "But if it came while he was in here with Grover—"

Luke's face was a cold, bitter mask. He nodded. "If Slim did this on his own, he's probably halfway to the Mexican Border."

Lafe asked: "We going after him?"

Luke shook his head. "Something bigger I've got to attend to first." His smile was thin. "But all trails cross sometime, Lafe; we'll run into Slim again."

He turned back to Fred. "We're looking for a man named Matt. He came in here this morning."

Fred licked his lips.

"You saw him?"

Fred nodded. He shot a look at Blake, rubbed a palm across his stubbled chin.

"He asked directions from Mister Grover. He was looking for Bert Foley's cabin."

Luke considered this, glanced at Red. "Those two old miners?"

Red nodded.

"How much of a ride?"

"Couple of hours," Red answered.

Luke's voice was bleak. "Let's go."

MATT VICKERS, slumped over his saddle horn, drifted into the alley alongside the sheriff's office, only half conscious of where he was. The ride from Foley's place seemed to have taken an eternity; he was only dimly aware of coming to the outskirts of Fulton. He made a desperate attempt to orient himself then, the sharp sense of danger pricking the blackness that swam before his eyes.

He slid out of the saddle in the alley and stumbled back toward the front of the law office. He had to find a place to stay, and instinctively he sought out Doc Emory.

The law office was unlocked, but even as he stumbled inside Matt knew there was no one else there. It was dark, and the recent rain had left a chill in the air. It *smelled* empty.

He whispered, "Doc!" a sick feeling gripping him. He had promised Doc he'd be back to face Luke McQuade, but he had the empty feeling now that he had come back too late.

He went outside and suddenly flattened against the blackness of the building as four riders went by, heading for the railroad station. He caught a glimpse of Luke's face, recognizing the outlaw. Matt waited until they had gone. Then he turned into the alley and climbed into the saddle again.

Doc Emory could be back in his room at the Standish House, but it would be too risky to try to find him there. Matt's numbed mind sought another solution. There was only one other place in town he could go.

He crowded the black horse into the shadows, slipping like a wraith through the muddy streets. The Grover cottage was on a side street, its yard shadowed by tall pecan trees.

Vickers rode into the yard and stopped under the trees. He left his reins trailing as he turned to the back door. He felt the blood start pounding in his head, felt the warm trickle of blood start down his caked cheek again.

It was an effort to reach the back door. He pounded on it, leaning against it as his strength started to drain from him.

After an eternity the door opened. He nearly fell inside, managing to cling to the framing.

Sarah's frightened face stared out at him.

He said, "Call Paul Grover. I'm a friend."

Sarah backed away from him. Matt moved inside, shoving the door shut behind him. He was in the Grover kitchen. The lamplight hurt his eyes, and he blinked. His head bandage was entirely red from seeping blood.

Sarah called out: "Betty!"

Betty came into the kitchen. She saw Matt, gave a gasp of surprise and went to him.

Matt forced a smile. "Sorry," he said slowly, "but this time I do need your help."

He started to sag. Betty and Sarah held him, turned him toward the living room.

Matt tried to hold onto his slipping consciousness. "Left my horse under the trees. Get him out of sight."

Betty nodded.

"Don't talk. Doctor Blake should be back soon."

Together, she and Sarah managed to get Matt to the sofa; he slipped into unconsciousness.

Slowly Betty straightened and turned to Sarah. "Get some water boiling. We'll do what we can for him until Doctor Blake gets here."

– XVI –

SUNSHINE MADE a pale splotch in the bedroom when Matt opened his eyes the next morning.

His head was clear, and he remembered where he was. His skull ached, but it was a dull, bearable pain. He could feel bandages around his head.

He sat up. He felt surprisingly strong, but the effort brought the pain over his temple into sharper focus. He squinted his eyes against the throbbing, and remembered Doctor Blake bending over him and, later, Betty. More vaguely he remembered talk of Luke McQuade and robbery and Paul Grover, disconnected fragments that he couldn't put together.

He was thinking about this when Betty came into the room, carrying a breakfast tray. She smiled as she saw Matt sitting up.

"You look much better this morning," she said.

"I feel much better," he answered.

"Feel like eating?" Her voice was cheerful enough. "Roger said it would be all right, if you felt hungry."

Matt nodded. "I'm starved."

She brought the tray over and set it on the covers in front of him. Her eyes had dark shadows under them, but her smile remained bright. "You're taking it much better than Dad."

The federal officer frowned. "Was he hurt?"

She nodded. "Slight concussion, Roger says." She sobered. "Dad was robbed of the railroad payroll last night. Roger found him lying in front of the safe, in the station. One of Luke's men, he thinks."

Matt drank his coffee. Doctor Blake came into the room and stood beside the bed, taking Matt's pulse. He looked tired, discouraged.

"Glad to see you up, Matt. Take it easy, though. That's an ugly wound you've got. A half-inch deeper—" He shrugged eloqently.

"Hazards of my job," Vickers said. He was thinking of Doc, wondering how the small man had fared.

"Guess I'm out of a job here," Blake commented wearily. "And so's Mr. Grover. The Desert Line's finished."

Vickers shrugged. "Why? Because of the stolen payroll?"

Blake made a tired gesture. "Oh, it's more than that. It's all the things that have happened." His voice turned bitter. "We just found out Mike Flannagan's dead. Mike was the track foreman at Track Town; it was Mike, mostly, who kept the men working on the line. Luke was up there the other day; he egged Mike into a fight and killed him. Then Luke frightened half the laborers away from the job, telling them the Desert Lines was broke and could never meet the payroll. The rest of the workers will follow when news of the payroll robbery gets back to them."

Matt pushed his tray aside. "Where's your father?" he asked Betty.

"In the next room." She hesitated. "Dad had all his savings tied up in the railroad. I think that's why he's taking it so badly."

Matt said, "I'd like to talk with him."

He waited until the girl left the room. Then he got up and put on his clothes. He felt somewhat light-headed, but the weight of the gun on his hip was reassuring. And a grim need was prodding him.

Blake eyed him with open respect. "Luke McQuade's searching all over town for you," he said slowly. "He knows who you are—Matt Vickers."

Matt was checking his gun; he nodded absently. There was no longer need to cover up.

Blake said, "They smashed up George Melvin's place, the *Gazette*. Gave him notice to get out of town." The doctor's voice was harsh. "Served the same warning on John Carlson." His lips twisted bitterly. "Luke could have saved his breath. Most folks will be leaving Fulton anyway."

Matt came up to him. "Where's Doc Emory, the man they hired on as town marshal?"

Blake frowned. "Was he a friend of yours?" At Matt's nod, he added, "I guess that's why Luke killed him, out in front of the Pecos Bar."

Matt was silent for a moment, absorbing the fact of the little man's death. Maybe Doc Emory had settled things with himself this way. Death was the final arbiter, after all.

A bleakness pinched Matt's face as he remembered his arrival in Fulton. Three of them—three outsiders riding for a showdown against Fulton's killers. Now only two remained.

Paul Grover was in bed. He pushed himself up to a sitting position when Matt walked in, followed by Betty and young Blake. He motioned Matt to a chair.

The United States marshal shook his head. "I've got to leave, Paul. But I came to ask you if you received an answer to my wire."

Paul nodded. "It came in last night. I started to copy it down, but one of Luke's riders was standing over me." He paused, remembering the message.

"Tom Billens had no brother."

"And the other?"

Paul frowned. "Chris Marlowe was not in Austin. No one knew where he was."

Matt nodded grimly, as though he had expected these answers. He turned away.

"Matt—" Paul's voice was harsh—"I haven't told anyone yet, not even Betty and Roger. But that payroll box I received last night—there was no money in it."

His voice held a flat, disillusioned note. "The iron box was filled with strips of old newspapers. I opened it just before I was knocked unconscious."

A deadly glitter came into the federal officer's eyes. He nodded. "Thanks, Paul," he said bleakly. "A lot of things make sense now." He turned away, a big, easy-stepping man with a thick white bandage around his head over which crisp black hair made a sharp contrast.

Betty stopped him at the door. "Matt, you're in no condition to go out. And Roger says that Luke McQuade is—" She faltered.

"I don't want to keep him waiting too long," Matt said grimly. Then he smiled and added gently: "Thanks for last night, Betty—and for everything."

He went out. Betty stared at the door. Blake moved up beside her, and she turned to him, a sob in her voice. "Oh, Roger—"

He took her in his arms, understanding, and not feeling jealous.

Death was abroad in Fulton this morning.

THE SUN was bright on the puddles in the street, reflecting a thousand spears of light against the drab, unpainted buildings. The wheels of passing vehicles churned deep through the mud.

Matt Vickers rode his big stud to the tie-rack before the sheriff's office and went inside. There was an emptiness in the office which seemed to voice mute questions; the open cell doors looked askance at him.

He stood by the spur-scarred desk and seemed to see Doc Emory's strained features behind it; the way Doc's fingers had rubbed the badge on his coat.

He was still standing there when Kip Billens came through the doorway. The youngster stopped short; for a brief moment he had the stark, surprised stance of a man staring at a ghost. His stogie dangled from his lower lip.

Matt looked at him. There was a silence in the office, heavy between them.

"Hello, Kip," Matt greeted him casually.

"They got Doc!" Kip said. His gloved right hand rubbed nervously over his Colt butt. "I wasn't around when it happened, or I would have helped. Luke came to town looking for you. He knew who you were. He got to Doc instead."

The U.S. marshal nodded. "I heard." His voice was level. "Doc was counting on you, Kip. Where were you?"

The cold-eyed youngster shrugged. He had recovered from his surprise. He held Matt's glance with cool steadiness.

"I went back to the hotel. You see, I didn't think Luke would be coming around so soon." His voice sounded defiant. "Doc could have stayed put, Matt. He didn't have to go out looking for trouble."

"It was his job," Matt reminded Kip grimly. "When he accepted that badge, it became his job to stop Luke."

Kip sneered. "Then he shouldn't have taken the job. He wasn't good enough to buck Luke McQuade, and he knew it."

"He tried!" Matt snapped.

"And got himself killed!" Kip's voice was curt, cynical, "It's your job, too, ain't it?"

Matt's eyes narrowed. "It is. But it seems I remember hearing you talk about how badly you wanted to come to Fulton. You said you were Tom Billens' brother. You sounded mighty anxious to get the men who killed him."

"I still want to!" Kip snarled. "But I'll do it my way, not Doc's way; not by stepping right out and facing Luke's guns. I ain't that good, Matt. And I want to stay alive while I do my job."

Matt eyed him with bleak contempt. "Then maybe you'd better stay behind. I've got Doc's job to finish, and my own."

Kip calmed abruptly. "Where are you going?"

"Across the bridge." Matt smiled coldly. "I hear Luke's been all over town looking for me. I want him to find me."

A strange flicker passed through Kip's eyes. "Well, I ain't that worried," he muttered. He looked sharply at Matt. "I told you in Paseo I was coming in with you. I still mean it. You're not Doc Emory. If anyone can buck Luke, you're the man."

"Thanks," Matt said dryly.

"I'm coming along."

Kip's hard face stiffened under Vickers' cold scrutiny. "Well?" he asked truculently.

Vickers walked to the desk and searched through the drawers until he found what he wanted: a deputy's badge. He tossed it to Kip.

"We may as well make it official," he said. His voice was faintly mocking. "Doc died wearing a badge. Maybe you'll do better."

Kip fingered the bright piece of metal, looking at it as though it were a strange toy. His grin was lopsided. He seemed to find an odd humor in the situation.

"Sure," he agreed. He pinned the badge to his coat and gave it a wipe with his sleeve. The gesture had something of ridicule in it, but Matt ignored it.

He had taken out his own badge and was pinning it to his coat.

"Let's go," he said curtly. "I've got a lot to do before night."

A small group was gathered on the walk outside the law office. John Carlson came pushing through them, heading for the door. He stopped short as Matt and Kip Billens came out.

Carlson pointed to the badge on Matt's coat.

"What is that, mister—a joke?"

Matt shook his head. "Sorry I couldn't tell you before, John, but I'm from the United States marshal's office. Matt Vickers. I'm taking over for Doc Emory."

Carlson followed them to the edge of the plank walk. "Where are you going?"

"I heard Luke McQuade hangs out in a place called the Gay Dog," Matt answered, and swung his mettlesome stallion away from the tie-rack.

Behind him, John Carlson stood a moment, like a man struck a surprise blow. Then he stepped off into the muck, unmindful of his polished shoes.

He had to see what happened. The future of Fulton was riding with these two men!

THE GAY DOG was seldom gay. It was strictly a drinking establishment, with a few tables for the inveterate card players. It stood somewhat apart from the other ramshackle structures, the nearest of which had already been abandoned by the itinerant citizens who had come to Fulton with the boom and read their interpretation of the town's future status when Sheriff Tom Billens had been killed.

Luke McQuade was hunched over a solitaire layout on a card table when Red Slater came inside, a cold urgency in his stride. He crossed to the table where Lafe and Bibs were standing watching Luke.

"He's riding in across the bridge," Red said, "like you said he would."

Luke nodded absently. He placed the black jack carefully under the red queen. Then he set the rest of his cards aside, like a man who expected to return shortly to finish his game.

"Push a man with a reputation hard enough," he murmured, "and sooner or later he'll come looking for you."

He stood up and gave a hitch to his sagging gunbelt. "No sense in messing up Art's place," he told his companions. "Let's go meet the marshal outside."

Lafe, Bibs and Red drifted toward the door behind McQuade.

Luke paused on the single wooden step under the Gay Dog sign and watched the two riders moving down the street toward him. Behind Matt and Kip trailed a small, cautious group of townspeople.

Matt Vickers! A man with a gun reputation

himself, Luke could appreciate that of the man riding toward him. Both men lived by their guns, but on opposite sides of the law fence.

He thought for a moment of his brother, and curiously, he felt no anger toward the marshal because of Ret.

Last night, a sense of loss had lashed him into trying to find Vickers. Now the marshal was only a man with a reputation as a fast gun, and Luke felt a strange elation at the approaching opportunity to test that reputation.

One of the men standing behind him said, "Who's the joker riding with him, Luke?"

Luke squinted slightly, studying Kip. He shrugged. "Don't know. You boys take care of him. I'll handle Vickers."

They stepped away from the Gay Dog now, the three men fanning away from Luke.

A hundred yards away, close to the spot where Doc Emory had died, Vickers reined his mount to a stop and dismounted. Kip slid out of the saddle and stood beside him. There was nothing left to say. What had to be said had been spoken. What lay ahead needed no telling.

The sun made a thousand sparkles on the muddy puddles between the two and the four men moving to meet them.

Luke was slightly ahead of the others, moving with that hunched-over walk of his. He was looking at Vickers with dark-browed casualness, looking at Matt's hands.

Luke was an old hand at gunplay.

Matt's stride was unhurried. He knew Luke was fast. How fast the next few seconds would tell. He felt neither fear nor apprehension in that tense moment, only a bitter urgency to get the showdown over with.

Luke's glance came up when they were less than fifty feet apart, and Matt drew at that hint of Luke's move. Vickers' Colt slammed two shots into Luke's chest as the outlaw slipped one wild shot high and whistling over Matt's head.

For a bare moment the outlaw boss stood stock-still after the first jerk of impact, stark surprise widening his eyes. Then he took a step forward, triggered an aimless shot into the dirt at his feet, and crumpled.

There had been a moment's hesitation on the part of the men with Luke; it was as though they had been waiting to see Luke's play through. Now they grabbed desperately at their holstered guns.

Matt's shot spun Red Slater around and dropped him. Kip's slugs smashed into Lafe a trifle belatedly, jerking the outlaw back and around, a blank look in his eyes. Then both lawmen's guns centered on Bibs, who was unnerved, shooting wildly; their shots dropped the long-rider face down into the puddle at his feet.

The scene had played itself out in a little more than thirty seconds. Kip stood slouched, his gun still smoking in his hand, staring with blank, stunned gaze at the killers sprawled in front of the saloon. Then he turned to face Matt and started slightly as he saw that Vickers' Colt, held loosely, was pointed at him.

He searched Matt's face and found nothing in it to reassure him. He said tightly, "Well, I guess Luke found you at that."

He holstered his Colt, and only then, casually, as if he had somehow forgotten, did Matt slide his gun back into the holster.

"I've got the rest of the job to finish," Vickers said. "You still want to ride along?"

Kip smiled, a thin, bleak-lipped smile. "You couldn't keep me away, Matt," he murmured.

They mounted and rode off before the small crowd straggled up. They didn't look back.

THE SUN slid down toward the western hills and ploughed into a mass of cottony clouds. Ahead of Matt and Kip, the country heaved up to the barren, broken Conchos. Red Canyon made a dark gap in the hills twenty miles away.

A ridge loomed up ahead, stippled with brush; a gully ran like a giant's nail, clawing through it.

This was the ridge on which Bert Foley had mentioned seeing the woman rider. It was time now, Vickers decided, to draw the joker from the pack.

He turned his stallion aside with an abrupt movement, jostling into Kip, and his Colt suddenly prodded into the gunster's side.

Kip jerked. "What the devil?"

"Shut up!" Vickers' eyes held a deadly glitter. He reached out and slipped Kip's Colt from the holster, flipped the cylinder out and jerked the bullet from it. Then he handed the empty gun back to the white-faced man.

"Always like to draw a rattler's fangs," he said coldly, "especially when I'm about to ride into a nest of them."

Kip's face distorted. "This is a heck of a time for a joke, Matt!" His voice was a puzzled snarl. "I stood by you back there, against Luke and his men."

"Sure you did," Matt admitted. "You had to make it look good, didn't you? But I noticed you waited until I stopped Luke before you took a hand."

"You gone crazy?" Kip's voice was shaken now. "Why would I want to do that? Luke killed my brother!"

"Tom Billens didn't have a brother," Matt interrupted. "I don't know who you are or how you talked Doc Emory into believing your story. But you're not Kip Billens."

The hard-faced killer shrugged. "Maybe not," he admitted. He forced a defiant sneer onto his pale face. "All right, so I'm not Tom Billen's brother. But you have nothing else on me, Marshal. I backed you up in town—there were more than twenty witnesses."

Matt's gaze dropped to Kip's hands. "You took to wearing gloves the morning the Barnes woman was smothered to death. It bothers me, Kip. I want a look at your hands."

Kip's eyes flamed with a thin, murderous light. "You can't hang that killing on me!"

The hammer of his gun clicked back under the U.S. marshal's thumb. "I intend to hang a lot of things on you," he growled. "Now peel them off!"

Kip's teeth showed against his drawn lips as he obeyed. Matt's eyes narrowed on the small, scabbed-over scratches.

"You told Doc and me that you had stepped out for a breath of air that night," Matt recalled grimly. "But you were in Vicki Barnes' bedroom, weren't you, while I was talking to her? You killed her right after I left, locked the door, and ducked out the back window and down the outside stairs."

"Go to blazes!" Kip exploded.

"You weren't with Doc yesterday afternoon, either," Matt continued harshly. "You followed me, didn't you, first to the railroad station, then to Bert Foley's shack?"

"You'll never prove that!" Kip snarled.

Matt shrugged. "We'll see." He made a motion with his Colt toward the ridge.

"We're going to meet your boss at Indian Tanks. I know there's a lookout on that ridge somewhere. What happens from here on in is up to you. We're going to ride toward that ridge with you holding that empty gun on me, or I'll kill you now and take my chances on getting past that lookout alone."

Kip licked dry, bloodless lips. "You wouldn't shoot me without giving me a chance?"

Vickers' gun muzzle regarded Kip with deadly impartiality. Above the blued barrel, Matt's eyes studied Kip with an uncompromising glitter.

"You choked a woman to death without giving her a chance. You didn't give Bert Foley and his partner a chance, either." Matt's voice was bleak. "You still think I wouldn't shoot you?"

It was a bluff, but it worked. Kip was the kind of man who would not have hesitated to kill, had the situation been reversed; he could believe Vickers meant exactly what he said.

He sagged in his saddle. "All right," he muttered. "I'll play it your way."

They were in the gully when the lookout appeared on the gray rock above them—a half-breed with a rifle.

Kip looked up and waved. "Jose, I'm coming in with a prisoner."

Jose waved them on.

They rode past, following the winding, narrowing gulch through the ridge, and emerged into a small, bowl-like valley hemmed in by hot bare hills. Ahead and below, on the small bench jutting across the valley, was the old Spanish camp Foley had described. Behind the ruins of the adobe barracks loomed a reddish slope, pockmarked with old mining shafts.

Four figures were standing in front of the main structure, which showed evidences of having recently been repaired to the point of habitability. Three of them were females; the other was a heavy-set man wearing a white sombrero.

He stood stock-still, the heavy gold chain looped across his vest glinting in the hazy sunlight. The cigar between his teeth drooped downward.

Matt and Kip rode up and pulled their animals to a halt a scant five paces away.

Matt's glance passed over the scowling man; it rested on the woman standing beside him for a brief moment. Then Vickers touched his hat in polite deference to her presence there.

"Hello, Chris," he said pleasantly to the big man. "I see you've found your wife and daughter."

Marlowe's cigar jerked. Mrs. Marlowe, a tall, graceful woman with white hair, smiled. "I believe I've seen you in Austin, haven't I? It's Matt Vickers. You're a United States marshal?"

Matt nodded. His glance made a swift appraisal of the fourteen-year-old girl standing beside her mother. With them was the fat Mexican cook who doubled as maid for the little group. It was evident that the Marlowe women had been quite comfortable there.

Marlowe found his voice. "Lou!" he snapped harshly at the still-faced killer. "Why did you bring him here?"

Kip said nothing. His face was like a gray mask; only his eyes watched Matt, alive and deadly.

"So his name is Lou," Matt muttered. "He didn't bring me here, Chris. I brought him."

Marlowe took a step backward, his eyes shifting, lifting to Jose's small figure coming down the slope toward them. Jose's rifle was tucked under his left arm.

"Why, what's wrong?" Mrs. Marlowe asked. Her innocence was too genuine; it surprised Vickers.

"I'm afraid there are a great many things wrong," Matt said. "I'd rather your husband told you, later. Right now I've come to bring him back with me to Austin, to explain to a lot of stockholders why he tried so hard to wreck his own railroad."

Marlowe's voice was a harsh whisper. "You know?"

Matt shrugged. "I put it together after I got an answer to my wire. An old prospector named Foley saw your wife up on the ridge, riding a white horse. You told everyone your wife and daughter had been kidnaped, that you had been threatened they would be killed if you didn't hold up building across the Strip." Matt shook his head. "Foley's story didn't jibe with that, Chris. The woman he saw on the ridge was riding free; she wasn't under restraint."

Marlowe's features sagged. "I thought I had taken care of you," he said. "Lou told me he killed you." Chris didn't notice the growing horror in his wife's eyes. "I knew I had to stop you when I found out you were being sent to Fulton. Luke McQuade might not be able to handle you; I got Lou here. It seemed foolproof. Lou worked on Doc Emory to come to town with you. He was to be my ace in the hole."

"Chris!" His wife's voice rang out sharply, unbelieving. "What are you saying? You told me threats had been made against you, against Lucy and me. You convinced me it would be best if we came here. You said it would be just for a little while, until the trouble with the railroad blew over. I can't understand! I can't—"

Marlowe stood like a man of stone. "A half-million dollars," he whispered. "I stood to make a half-million—stockholders' money—when the Desert Line went into bankruptcy."

Kip made his break then. He kneed his horse savagely into Matt's mount, whirled away, and yanked his rifle free. He swung the muzzle around toward Vickers and levered off one shot before the marshal's return fire lifted him out of the saddle. He crashed heavily on his back, and his big bay, stepping back with a mincing, frightened gait, stepped on Kip's upturned, twisted face.

Mrs. Marlowe screamed and turned away. Matt

backed his horse around, away from Chris, to face the lookout.

Jose was running toward them now, his rifle coming up. Matt's bullet kicked up dirt at Jose's feet in a grim warning. Jose stopped.

"Chris," he snapped to the big railroad man, "don't make me kill him!"

Marlowe took a deep breath. He raised his voice and yelled out in Spanish, "Drop it, Jose. I don't want any more killing."

He stood there in the dying sunlight, the ruddiness gone from his face—a big man who had played a ruthless game for high stakes.

By his side, his wife's sobbing made a harsh sound in the stillness. Her daughter was holding her, not crying, not quite understanding. The Mexican woman stood helplessly by, moaning softly.

Slowly Matt slid his Colt back into his holster. There was an echoing sadness in him as he listened to the woman crying.

Finally he said, "It's a long way back to Austin, Chris. I think we better get moving."